AUTOMAT PRESS
Berlin, Germany

Edited and designed by Thomas Huntington

ISBN: 9780645795899

KIMBERLEY *of* WALKAWAY

IAN HORROCKS

CHAPTER ONE

I dig my heels in

That Sunday. The middle of a long friendless summer. Climate change meant the pre-wet normally expected up north had drifted south, we were unused to it. Like the approaching stormy weather this moment had been brewing for weeks. I knew when that moment arrived it would be impossible to avoid. I wanted it to happen, to finish the whole business.

Summer were always long: but long and bone dry. This north-west weather, with its intolerable humidity had lasted for weeks, its intolerable humidity gripping the property. Like the shirts stuck to our backs, which left white, salty crusts on the khaki when they dried overnight: the cyclone season would make its mark.

I'd just become a 13 year old.

Gabby was no use, not yet even eleven, and we had no conversation anyway, then once invited south she'd been allowed to go. With no close friends to invite over, once School of the Air was closed for summer break and my usual radio buddies escaped, 2000 kms south. Down to a cool, full of friends, beach holiday.

Unless I made sure I rode out by dawn, it was too hot for a long ride. Anyway, I had no one to ride with. Then, later in the day any horse asked to traverse the parched, cracked clay would have burned their feet. Steel horseshoes sucked up heat, blistering even the tough shell of horse hooves.

Every farm track was baked hard. Both red pindang clay and black swamp clay had begun cracking under the dryness. Only a single tree had somehow remained slightly green, everything else in the homestead garden had drooped or had leaves so frizzled they'd turned cinnamon brown. Even the tough, desert hardy, eucalypts, which rimmed the homestead perimeter, were sighing with exhaustion before night. In the darkness came gunshots: sounds of their branches snapping before crashing to lay in the dust.

Water became such a scarce commodity. Mum ceased watering the pool lawn. Our usually sparkling blue, turned turgid, becoming a slimy green. A horrible job, waiting until the season broke and ample water returned. Our usually verdant pool-lawn was so dead I couldn't cross it in bare feet, yellowed blades of dry grass prickled the scorching heat through my boot soles.

Family conversation dried up. Any time I made small talk, I found myself in strife.

I'd never had more than flippant arguments with my beloved Poppa, now every time we talked it was me who unearthed the bone of contention. I couldn't understand what had changed so much.

Not only had the days of stinking hot weather gone on and on and on and on, but every night had also become so hot and so humid our entire household had shifted bedrooms, out onto camp beds on the verandahs. Everyone sheltered under a simple cotton sheet or net covering. Mosquito bites turned septic and wept if you scratched them.

I felt lonely and unloved, a mosquito searching for someone to bite.

My entire family became bad tempered, for inexplicable or unwarranted reasons. I was as ill-tempered as the others, much of each day spent in pointless argument.

***

A rare, slow, cool breeze chilled me, waking me early. Rather than get up or pull up a blanket, I tucked my head under my arm, smelling an unfamiliar scent. Not the sweaty smell associated with Dad, or the fire-smoky smell of the Aboriginal staff: not unpleasant but new. Both armpits smelt the same.

Showers were necessarily short, but I used litres of precious water to have a quick lukewarm one before crawling back into bed. Soap removed it. By night, it was back. I asked Mum, 'It comes with the other changes to your body after beginning menstruation; just use a deodorant.'

My smelly armpits were no concern compared to all the other problems she had: but it was my newest and biggest problem. I used most of her stick of roll-on and it disappeared, replaced by the smell associated with my mum after showers.

Just another aggravation, but with no friends to talk with about it. I desperately wished Harry was still around; he may be a boy, but he'd have listened and understood. No one else had time.

***

This looked increasingly like being one dull, dry, dusty, khaki-coloured and unbearably long summer with no one to complain with and not even a bright green tree to gaze longingly at. Days and nights stuffed full of endlessly rasping, blunt edged cicadas. Every day too long, too humid, too hot as the whole world became arm-pit smelly. The homestead became full of sharp grey corners, the three long verandahs overcrowded with bunk beds, every door to every bedroom thrown open. All opened onto the same cluttered verandah, in futile attempts to catch a nonexistent breeze; attracting giant mosquitoes instead. I couldn't even roller-blade to generate my own small breeze.

With no wood fire or good cooking smells to salivate on, mum's kitchen offered little comfort. Our toilets were suddenly narrow, dark and filled with awful smells. My bedding began absorbing my new odour, my undies drawer constantly empty and out of clean t's. My clothes basket had begun to attract attention.

***

My bedroom mirror developed a green slime. I began to think my skin had actually turned a shade of green when I looked into it. I was being ignored by Dad any time a job needed doing. Something had to happen. Someone had to break the spell, lift the siege, create a diversion.

So I did.

CHAPTER TWO

The storm breaks

'Dad' I yelled as he walked from the verandah, intensely angry at how he ignored me. 'Don't you dare just walk off. I want to help you. Just because Harry's headed north doesn't mean you, me, and Gabby can't become a new team, or can you only work with men?' realizing as I spoke I was almost yelling.

He stopped in his tracks, twenty steps away. I continued. Speaking to his sweat-crusted shirt back because he hadn't turned around. 'Just because compared to you I'm a little, pimply-faced girl doesn't mean I can't do most things round here. One day I will be grown up, and you will be old, and Harry will still be up north. Then who will look after Walkaway?' voice still rising. 'It's a Sunday but I'm here ready to work!'

I figured he was at least listening, so I ploughed on, my pitch rising with each sentence. 'If you eased up for a moment and bothered to actually look at the paddock-books, you'd see most recent entries were entered by me, not Mum. If you checked Bert's old ute you'd see I did the oil change, the one you never got round to and, if you looked at the Yammy, you might notice I managed to fix the busted chain, without help from either you or Harry. Then if you took a bit more time and bothered to look at the skills chart Poppa drew up, the one he did so I'd be sure to have every skill I needed to run Walkaway; you'd seen almost all the boxes are already ticked,' pausing for breath something sank in, I realised I'd unintentionally raised my voice to a shout. What had started out to be just a loud 'look at me' had become a one lonely girl shouting match, I hadn't realised how much frustration was pent up.

He turned to face me, but I was on a roll and still pretty angry so decided to keep yelling, it was fun, 'I'm not a baby, you know. I'm almost thirteen and can do just about everything Harry used to. Your other daughter Gabby is eleven and pretty competent too, so why is it you always found time to talk to number one son Harry about each day's work and give him a list of jobs, but not us? We sit at the same breakfast table, Gabby feeds the same chooks and I milk Bessie, usually before you're even up, school day or not. We don't take lazy days like you once the harvest is done. So unless deep down you really think girls are second-class members of this family, we deserve your attention!' knowing as I blurted it that my anger and frustration had taken me a step too far.

Thank heavens I took another breath and stopped, because I heard the screen door bang shut and knew Mum had stepped onto the verandah right behind me.

'Maybe it's time the remaining members of this family had a talk about things, Brad,' she murmured softly. 'Perhaps a second cup of tea wouldn't go astray,' padding back inside in her flip-flop thongs.

Dad lumped up the steps to where I still stood with only one boot on, the other still in my hand. He looked so crestfallen I hopped over and hugged him. I desperately needed him to understand I wasn't angry with him, just frustrated and deeply upset at how he'd been treating me since Harry left.

Even in my frustration and anger, I'd guessed he probably couldn't see that.

I was instantly sorry for what I'd just said. I walked behind him into the kitchen, head not quite hanging down.

Gran, bent double over the table as we walked in, twisted to see.

Mum already had the teapot out, five mugs around a plated pile of yesterday's cold buttered scones on her hand-painted plate. 'Gob-fillers' Gran long ago called them, 'something to shove in your mouth when you're about to say something you might regret later': her comment instantly came to mind.

The day was hot and sticky, but through the door I noticed the damper on the Aga was fully open. If someone didn't close the damper, there was a fair chance it would burn the bottom out of another kettle.

I had no idea who'd lit it or why, but like me, morning fires can get a bit of a go on if you don't watch out.

Dad plonked awkwardly at his end of the table as Mum poured his cuppa, keeping the big aluminium pot in front of her, her lips dry and thin as two blades of second-grade straw. Gabby, notably absent, was apparently still catching up on her beauty sleep; it was Sunday after all, and a girl's gotta catch her z's when she can.

Through her warm, constantly runny eyes, Gran stared across at her big son, the shape of her ancient mouth drifting as it wandered between a smile and a glare. I figured it was up to me; it was me who started it, though I knew Sis and Harry supported me. As it dawned on me my mouth had also become bone dry, I reached to pick for the teapot, for a lip-wetting cup of hot tea.

Embarrassingly, given the tension, the milk jug was down at Dad's end. 'Can you pass me the milk Dad?' almost as an afterthought, 'please'.

Without looking up, he scooted it toward me. 'I guess I should start,' he grumbled softly, 'It's really me that's in strife here, not you Splinter, you just had the courage to say what no one else could, so good on you.'

Gran looked at me with her increasingly lopsided, wicked old grin, which even as it slipped sideways across the rugged landscape of her face still had the ability to make me feel comfortable. No matter how bad things were, I could usually be certain Gran would muster a gentle grin. This time her words were as gentle as ever, 'I think maybe we all should apologise to Splinter for making her carry the rubbish bin out'.

Sometimes she was with us, sometimes she was off with the fairies; today we shared her with the fairies. Across the table Mum smiled sadly at me.

'I'm sorry, darling. I had noticed and should have said something before Harry left. You leave words unsaid long enough, they often never find the courage to crystalise, unless someone forces them out. Three weeks is too long.' reaching to hold my hand across a corner of the table.

As Dad reached out from the other side, I put my cuppa down.

We sat quietly for a bit, till Gran made a noisy slurp as she drank her still too hot tea.

It broke the silence.

We all took a sip.

'Dad, I'm sorry, I shouldn't have yelled at you. It's not how I've been taught to discuss things.'

From across his steaming cuppa came a warmer glance than I'd seen for weeks, 'No, it's my fault things got to this stage, Splinter.' By the nickname he used I immediately knew he'd changed gear.

'It's taken you to wake us up. We all miss Harry. Me probably most of all, I'd always hoped he'd take over from me one day.'

Instantly my ire rose, attached to a change in colour of my neck, but before I could get stuck into that argument Mum leapt in

'No-one else can take that prize,' she smiled, 'I miss his craziness, his hugs every morning and him kissing me goodnight.'

Sure they could all see the wetness happening around my eyes. I paused before I spoke. 'I suppose you think I don't miss his craziness.'

Into the momentary silence Gran whispered again, 'Well, if we're all playing 'I miss' then I bags missing his gentle rub of my shoulders every time he walked past.'

Three hands reached across the table for a scone, tears close to the waterline in everyone's eyes. Reaching to choose the same brown-crusted one, Dad and I helped break our tension, hands touching over the same cold, slightly burned one.

Glancing up, I caught a sight of him I'd never seen before. His face had aged quickly. It looked tired, sagging further than I recalled, his left eyelid drooping more than I remembered. Years before he'd had a slight 'turn', as he called it, his left eye suffered most from the mini stroke, but today his skin had also lost its sun-burned vibrancy, now crusted with hard grey whiskers, flakey bits of skin around his prominent nose. I realised he was getting older, much older, much faster than Mum.

Gran took the floor again. For as long as I could remember, there'd often been a strangeness about her. During her long periods of silence, she would stare away, to some distant horizon, before snapping back into the conversation, as if she'd been talking to someone else. Tired or not, at night Mum would scold her to bed early. She never demurred, just levered herself up, lowered her head and shuffled down the hall, strangely crestfallen. She wouldn't say a word. Gabby followed to brush her hair. In the years before her marbles all began rolling into the dark recesses of her mind, Gran gave wise counsel, especially when things got rough, so she could still be certain of a more than generous silence each end of when she spoke.

This morning her crusted voice owned the floor, 'This daughter of yours can do everything Harry's taught her and do them well. He taught her a jolly lot too, including those mechanical skills you and Poppa never got round to. Since she was about three Beryl had taught her cooking. Gabrielle is to milk the Bessie. She stopped talking for a long-time, staring at Dad. 'These comments come from someone 'as seen this family misjudge too many people and too many events. Just don't underestimate her son!'

Ending her lecture, my father Gran looked directly at me, one of her huge warm smiles, giving me the courage to speak again.

'Dad, I know you always wanted a son to take over, but you only had one and though he tried hard to fit your mould and find a future here, now Harry wants a different life, up in new country. For as long as we've talked, he's wanted to give the northwest a go. Your family roots were up there, before something forced you to shift us all down here and you to become a wheat-cocky. You of all people should understand how he feels. Gabby and I may both share the same genes as Harry, but we both love the feel of warm grain running through our fingers, straight out of the harvester, Harry never caught that germ, he's a genuine Kimberley kid and needs the smell of cow shit up his nose'.

I looked across, Dad was listening, 'We've been down south so long, Gabby and I only want to stay in the wheatbelt, then take over here when you retire. I'm never running away to chase some other dream, and though I know high school will be difficult for a few years, I'll be home for the holidays. Please, just give me half a chance,'

Hearing the choke in my pleading.

He looked up, smiling limply. 'Porridge, I know you're a good worker, I know you're a quick learner, but you have no idea how hard it is to run this place,' all said with such a straight face it would have made me crack up, if he didn't have a history of being so bloody patronising. Before I could erupt into an argument, Mum interjected, raising the stakes further. 'How come she's missed noticing that? She's been here as long as the rest of us.'

The accuracy of her shot dropped a black mantilla of silence over the tea break.

Thank heavens Gabby chose that second to stroll in, looking for her late breakfast, in baggy jim-jams, hair sleep-tousled, beautiful eyes still gummy. She'd have needed to be deaf, dumb, and blind to miss the thick silence and downcast heads. She didn't need an excuse. 'Oops, maybe I should just go back to bed and come down in a half hour,' her levity breaking the tension.

Still searching for the right marble, Gran took another noisy sip of her still too-hot black tea. 'What if you write the lass a list, son. It might be a good idea to write it on the school blackboard, before the teacher gets here. List all the things you reckon she might need to learn to pass grade five. If you work on it together it might help improve your handwriting too.' As she drifted back to lala land Mum butted in, ignoring her foolish comment, talking directly to Dad.

'Kimberley's only here a few more weeks, then she's away to first term at high-school wherever that might finally be. I want to spend as much time with her as I can and you might as well get some mileage out of her, before you've only got Bert to boss around.'

***

Later that day I took the opportunity to ride with Dad, as he inspected the water tanks. Unlike me, he's always had the ability to switch off his shitty moods. He was again the exceptionally interesting father he'd always been, no sign of the stick in the mud of the morning.

I'd also cooled.

Riding around with him, I'd learnt the way he saw our country. Most trips he would stop, struggle out of the big dent where his seat had long ago collapsed, climb out, walking a few steps to bend and delicately collect the skeletal remains of some small creature, or the minute flower of an ephemeral plant or a chip of interesting rock. Long before I realised it, that was the way he'd ignited the perennial flame of inquiry I so liked about myself. No matter how small, every jewel was carried all day on the middle seat in the cabin, then brought inside at night, when over dinner he'd explain their unique story with a passion that was infectious, leaving knowledge and memories long remembered.

***

I'd gone with him hoping and expecting he would talk about Harry going north, or the problems he'd hinted my big brother might encounter; but no. In the back of my mind, I considered asking questions about how he saw the farm evolving with Harry gone, but it was still too complicated; he'd just have got upset. So I sat and enjoyed the warm feelings I always get when I'm out with him, no longer angry about how he saw me. I'd left that in the kitchen with the remaining scone, to resume the fight when I might have more chance of a win.

CHAPTER THREE

Walkaway and my folks

I can't be the only teenage girl who dreams of a future earning her living from the land, yet is frustrated by the attitude of older males in her family. I have such a clear view of what I want, and a family history of extracting living from the soil, I reckon it's worth telling my story.

Home now is Walkaway, fifty thousand hectares of cereal and sheep country, about an hour out of Mingenew, in Midwest Western Australia. Walkaway supports Mum, Dad, my little sis Gabrielle, and Gran, plus when he was still at home, my brother Harry. Harry's name has come down the male line, ever since Dad's Granddad, the first to wear the moniker.

Poppa used to work here too, but had to accept another offer: he left us to plough heaven's pastures.

Walkaway came down the female line. Dad's really just a caretaker not an operator. Gran's family originally bought and developed it as a staging point for fattening Kimberley beef, to get the best price at Perth markets. Much later, once live cattle began to be shipped out of Broome it languished, rather than sell we rented it to share-farmers who paid a regular rent.

That was until disaster struck up north. Following a fantastic wet season, when our cattle couldn't eat the buffel grass it grew so fast; came disaster. Our station was belted, buffeted and burnt, suffering badly from towering clouds infused with lightning, storms that ignited grass fires which burned uncontrolled for weeks, destroying most of the dry but still very edible buffel casually incinerating much of our herd.

The devastation of fire almost immediately followed by a monumental wet season with memorable downpours causing massive damage to the few remaining fences causing such losses to our remaining herd we had nowhere else to turn: but Walkaway.

Today, in return for providing our living, the grain farm that is Walkaway demands a different and solid performance from us all, requiring us to learn a new set of skills, except for Gran, who became strangely more silent and less communicative after the shift.

When we first came south she stayed living with Poppa, only shifting to live with us after he died of a stroke. Very suddenly she became very old. Her previously thick, lustrous, dark hair began thinning rapidly, in that horrible way some old ladies' hair does, to the point where you could suddenly see her liver spotted, pink skull-skin.

The loss of her hair upset her each night. Sis carefully brushed it for one hundred strokes to make it grow, but instead Gran watched her pride and joy become grey magpie nest-lining, stuck in the hairbrush.

Luckily she could not see our view of the top.

Her knees and wrists became arthritic too soon. To ease her pain both the house fire and the old wood-fired kitchen Aga now burned all through autumn and winter, except during this humid summer, when it would have been unbearable. Feeding the Aga's voracious appetites meant endless wood collecting and chopping. It was so just as well Walkaway had hectares of former woodlands still littered with dead timber.

Harry used to do the wood jobs and left a good pile, but it'll soon fall to Dad or me to keep it topped up. Because I hate chain sawing and chopping wood and slim Gabby could not manage to lift a chainsaw I'm desperately trying to think who else might do it. I don't mind carrying the baskets-full indoors, or dumping armloads from the trailer into the battered wood box on the back porch, but keeping the flow up will only work while I'm still at home.

Mum and Dad simply have not got the time spare. To me cutting wood is a man's work, with women just responsible to use it efficiently in the kitchen.

Like Mum does.

Cold wet weather aggravates Gran's hands more than her knees. She can tell ahead of time when a thick, damp sea fog will roll in. The afternoon before one arrives she begins to 'get the creaks', as she calls the painful aches that beset her hands.

'I've had the rheumatics so long I've learnt short cuts for most kitchen jobs, but the garden gets me' she mutters softly, while doped up on pain killers she helps around the house. So gardening falls by the way when the temp drops, unless Mum is there to help Gran in and out of her plastic kneeling frame, with its foam kneeling pad.

This scorching yet humid weather seems to have lessened her pain, about the only good thing about it.

Our house, as we call the homestead, was originally very small, just two rooms. A stone cottage, tiled with a roof of Blackbutt shingles, split from timber off the block. Four generations, plus share-farmers morphed it into what looks a bit like a shed with warts. Rooms sprouted organically off the square original hut, bulging into previously empty spaces so it now sprawls onto wide, tin-roofed verandahs, sheltering each side, except the east.

Off the south-west corner are the old long-drop toilets, which still work but aren't much used, except if you're outside and need to go in a hurry. They're plumbed now so are not really long-drops, but the old name sticks. We've installed plumbed inside toilets so the two off the verandah we now call the dunnies.

Out next to them I built a rather rough wire-mesh cage, which two injured cockies now call home. The spectacularly handsome bird is a Sulphur-Crested Cockatoo, the much less attractive one is a red-eyed, Long-beak Corella.

Originally scrubby bush with few water holes, generations of grain farmers have cleared it, excavated dams, and drilled bores to put in more water points, in order to sow more crops and graze sheep and cattle. Along the way they removed bird habitat while providing new food and water sources for them.

Where the vast flocks of cockies hibernate in the off season I don't know, but somewhere there must be a big sign advertising 'Camp Walkaway', because we've become a harvest season holiday camp to sky-filling flocks. Thousands of raucous white birds descend into crops to feed, creating havoc and bringing grief to our yield.

Dad mutters, 'I understand every cockatoo was created as part of the good lord's window dressing, but did he need to design them to be naturally destructive? It's just one of his angry epithets whenever our sky turns white, as if seeking some sort of divine apology for their existence. 'Ok they evolved those huge beaks to shred hollows in dead trees, to create safe nesting sites and to open hard seed cones, but when evolution was mucking with them I wasn't growing crops. When it comes to my crops they can go to hell, with my shotgun to assist them catch the first flight out.'

It's pointless to draw attention to the penalties for shooting protected birds.

It's illegal to keep them, I can legally keep them only because I found both as pin-feathered chicks, fallen out of hollow-limb nests, before they were fledged. Both fell in the same storm, each arrived home with a broken wing-bone, meaning they'd never be able to fly, more likely to become a midnight snack for some feral cat.

'I suppose they can't do much more damage now,' Dad mumbled when I sought his permission, presenting helplessly cradled in my hands two pin-feathered, ugly as sin, pink-skinned chicks, fat beaks almost covering their bug-eyed faces.

'I'll help feed them.' Softie Gran offered, 'They'll need feeding when you're at school. I doubt your teacher would let you have them in class.' It was a chore above and beyond the call of either duty or family. With an eye dropper and a mash made of bran and pollard, plus a dash of charcoal to stop them scouring, we shared the job, but on cold, damp days just squeezing the dropper hurt Gran's rheumatic fingers so much you could hear her wincing.

Until they were fully fledged, the pleasure of cleaning up their endless runny white poos remained totally my responsibility. Mostly Gran remembered her chore but sometimes I arrived home to their hungry chorus, luckily I loved playing mummy bird, feeding mash into wide-open, squawking, huge-beaked mouths.

Watching them grow each day noting grey pin feathers sprout, longer and thicker, until they blossomed into the purest whitest feathers, gave me total joy. Not until I'd trained them to patiently sit and shit on my shoulders after spending all day in a budgie cage, did Dad allow me to build the big bird cage.

Ok, it's a bit roughly put together, but it's also out of sight, in a spot where few except Poppa ever go near. I wanted them close and sheltered so I had little choice.

Unfortunately both birds screech when they want attention, which is every-time someone walks by, so it's become a pretty awful spot to go near, but I've had the utter delight of daily watching them grow to adulthood. Seeing pin feathers changing from black/grey, gradually sprouting into pure white, strong, purpose designed feathers for the flying my two would unfortunately never know, was informative and wonderful.

Long before he died Poppa named them.

Cockytoo and Cockyone. At his funeral, just as Gabby was asking where Poppy's spirit had gone after he died, a vast flock of snow-white Sulphur-crested's flew shrieking over the cemetery. Only half-joking Dad pointed up and told her, 'He's probably joined one of the bloody great cloud of Cockythrees and Cockyfours, teaching them some more fart jokes.' Gran's gentle admonition ricocheted back, 'Poppy sent them over just to make sure we remember him each time some fly past.'

Cockytoo the Sulphur-Crested is the way better talker, imitating everything even if he only hears it a couple of times, he's such a clever student he even gets accents and emphasis correct.

Because of his huge feet Dad has perennial trouble taking his boots off, so often swears when he comes onto the verandah at the end of a day in the paddocks, and guess who's sitting listening. Cockytoo can now swear really well, in the same broad Aussie accent as Dad.

Cockyone's laugh is so like Mum's shriek I sometimes have to stop and consider whether it could be her, coming in from the garden and walking along the verandah, or not. Cockyone and Mum share a laugh you never forget, but I can't imagine how Cockyone imitates her so accurately. Mum's comes from her belly, maybe because she was once skinny, it starts as a giggle then develops into a shriek, which ends up with her shaking all over.

How Cockyone does it from such a small frame bewilders me.

Cockytoo's funniest imitation comes when he flushes the outside dunny. Poppa always goes does toilet on the dunny each morning after breakfast, with Cockyone obviously listening for years. The bird imitation starts with a long burbling noise like a wet fart, then you hear Poppa's sigh. 'Aahh that's better!' then there's a short silent pause before you hear Poppa's voice again, 'Bugger, I can't reach my strides.'

If you stop laughing, a few seconds later you hear him reach the pull-down chain, followed by a clank, then the water flushes.

Visitors crack up whenever Cockyone performs the ritual. Needless to say Mum finds the whole thing disgusting.

After Poppa died last year, Gran stayed on in their house for a bit until Mum decided she was lonely and not eating well enough. Gran was the last surviving oldie of a northwest pastoral family who once owned several vast stations, each bigger than a million acres. She now just sighs that she really loves what she calls our little farm. It's the last of what she and my parents call 'the old history'.

Pop dying brought me to the first big financial decision of my life. He willed me his portion of everything he owned. His money does not resolve my grief. I miss him a lot, we were such good mates and there were still heaps of skills he never got around to teaching me. Gran's comments when I mention how I feel are so accurate. 'We never really use our time up with nice folk, yet waste so much with other not such nice ones, then look back when it's too late and wonder why.'

Mum's much younger than Dad and comes from an old wheatbelt farming family, all now left farming. One by one we've purchased their blocks as they left farming and the district. An avid member of the local CWA, when someone's in trouble Mum's amongst the first to lend a hand, whether by cooking crock-pots of hearty stews that will keep while baby-sitting or by nursing one while that family get on with farming.

We've learned to advise callers, 'We've lent Mum to someone temporarily less fortunate, we can put you on her to do list tho,' while we sit around a much quieter dinner table, eating cold leftovers, trying not to complain. Walkaway is what's called a mixed farm. We grow wheat and oats and raise Merino sheep for meat and medium strength wool plus a handful of Red Illawarra cows for our own consumption and for milk. An Aussie breed they're dual purpose meat and milk. With a wide range of work needed we can easily switch jobs.

Mum's elder sister Meryl married Dad's older brother Mort. So Beryl and Meryl married Brad and Mort. Photos from the joint wedding clearly show Mum far was younger and much slimmer. She is still much, much slimmer because Auntie

Meryl 'Just kept on growing into her skin,' Dad laughs 'and I suspect she'll find a few more wrinkles to fill up yet!'

Dad at two point two metres is huge, muscular and wiry all at once, so hardly 'normal'. Fit that bulk around a set of broad shoulders and a bull neck and he's pretty intimidating. Photos showed he didn't stop growing until he was in his twenties and even down in the Wheat-belt, where farmers grow as tall as their crops, Dad stands out in every crowd.

He was christened Harrold, the second son of an earlier Harrold, born into a then financially and socially important West Australian pastoral family. Despite being christened that no one ever called him Harrold. His second name was Bradley and that's what stuck.

Poppa used to explain it by saying, 'That family was so tight they were unwilling to even let go of a name once it worked but your Dad liked Bradley better and he won.'

By the time Dad was an adult his family had slowly and occasionally spectacularly lost almost everything, except Walkaway. plus a tenuous leasehold on Warra. Despite numerous tales of constant hard work and stories of long, long hours it seemed the family had continued taking chances on seasons and markets, and too many of their guesses were wrong.

***

If he was asked, Dad gave little away about the family's really major loss and didn't whinge about what might have been, only occasionally giving clues to how he felt. Harry and I kept wondering about the old business.

Mum says Dad has the stoic gene and Harry's inherited it too. Like when Harry said he was pulling up stumps to head north Dad didn't try to stop him, despite the extra pressure not having him would generate. The nearest I recall him making a comment came as we were all sitting around a big fire in the main lounge. It erupted after a memorable feast of roast beef and veg, with a steamed pudding for dessert. Such a vast and tasty meal even Auntie Meryl had been drawn to comment, 'Don't make meals like that anymore, sister,' wiping her dinner plate of the remnant thick brown gravy, with a crust of Mum's bread baked from our own wheat, before as she often did, punctuating her comment with a huge belch for the full stop.

For anyone else such an impolite act, yet for Aunt Meryl such a common thing, that no one even raised an eyebrow. But later when she wiped her pudding plate with her index finger, then licked it, before wiping it on the hem of her dress, Mum had the manners to look away.

Despite a damp ocean fog that had persistently refused to lift, maybe because of the thin sun being well past the top, Meryl and Mort left just an hour and a half after lunch, to drive the two hours back to the city.

Depending on our age, dinner had left us stuffed and sitting quietly, reading or dozing by the fire, so the sound of Dad grunting, 'Son, I truly envy you' shocked us all as it erupted into the warm silence. He continued in a clear voice, 'I envy your courage stepping into the unknown and I really envy you the future you'll find,' then paused for more than a breath, 'but just don't believe the bullshit you might hear,' pushing himself out of his armchair as he spoke.

Gran's gentle snoring was suddenly loud in the shocked silence that followed Dad's uncharacteristic outburst and the questions it raised. Despite that he was leaving the next day Harry obviously hadn't expected it either. Dad had never been given to long emotive speeches. 'Well done,' was an average length comment, 'flaming well done,' almost a biblical length exposition. Mostly he simply handed out jobs lists that required little or no explanation.

Everyone except Gran stopped what they were doing, to listen and watch.

As he walked to the liquor cabinet and poured a shot glass of whiskey Dad seemed unaware of the impact of his few words. It was not unusual for him to have a nip after a meal but unusually this time he did not ask if anyone else wanted to join him. Seated again he raised his glass for a sip before he fired his second salvo into the room, by then becoming full of a silence which I could feel deepen with each word he muttered. 'If folk find out who you are you might hear stuff that's not nice. A few others got singed, not just us, so it might be safer to use Mum's surname.'

Harry looked as if he'd been hit with a pick, his face instantly contorted in disbelief at what Dad had suggested, but he had little time to say anything as Dad went on, apparently oblivious to the muck he'd stirred up.

'You don't ever need to own up to being related to me,' neither smirking, scowling or even looking toward Harry. Mum noticeably tucked her head down, to focus on her knitting, Gran drifted into awake, smiling weakly, probably not yet fully comprehending what was happening, while Harry, Sis and I just stared.

'Old business' was almost never discussed in front of us so we had no solid clues as to what had transpired, exactly when, who had been involved, or where the once fabulous family fortune had vanished to. We knew there had once been both a huge fortune and more properties, in the days before a second cattle drive had pushed out into the desert. Photos on the hall wall had always attested to that. But if a question came up that required going back to that time Dad would look away and just mutter,'Old business,' with a pained expression and that would be the end of it.

From the look on Mum's face she knew what he was alluding to and obviously Gran must also have known. Harry spoke with a courage I didn't have and asked the question to which he and I had always wanted the answer.

'Is it time I knew?' he asked, from what you just said it sounds like it might be useful to know which rocks to leave unturned and which stumps to leave laying in the fallow paddock, if I want to avoid getting my head punched in'.

It felt as if a pulse in the room none of us had been aware of had quickened.

I noticed even Gran sat up a little straighter.

Dad took two slow sips of his Scotch, before his reply rumbled up and he answered in a voice which remained dry and rusty. 'It was not all of my doing, and parts of what went wrong pain me even now sitting here. Not saying I would have done things differently, but I was still only a kid.'

He stopped completely, looked first at Gran, then across at Mum, his face giving nothing away, before he continued. 'A thousand miles away from where he'd camped us, with the mob there'd been a fierce blow, must have been a huge dump of rain, but we heard and saw nothing of it,' he paused, 'the creek came up silently, suddenly, sudden as can be.' His voice faltered as he stared off into the distance, his scotch forgotten. 'The stock as was lost would've been part of my inheritance so it might've been nice to have had more of a say in setting up camp. But Dad was sometimes inclined to belt the bottle a bit, and if he had a bit of turps in him what he said always went, unless you wanted to find yourself flat on your back with a fat lip.'

No one knew who to look at, as Dad continued to stare at some distant horizon.

Harry prodded the fire and stared into it. Sis, on the floor next to him curled tightly, looking at no one, while I stared open mouthed at the man I most admired in the whole world, wondering what secret he had kept so tight for all my life.

Was that a thin whisk of smoke curling from its edges, the start of something.

Each sip took him closer to continuing. I don't think he needed the courage it would give him, he just had to break an old ugly habit of silence about that time of his life. It must have felt like the Mafia code of Omerta, 'speak the truth on pain of death'.

The strain in his face told us it was so patently painful it was hurting him. His skin had become more drawn, his forehead pulled down into uncharacteristic creases, his usually fly-proof mouth hung open and loose, silently staring into his almost empty glass, he went on quietly.

'The weather, it would be easy to blame it on the weather, but what came wasn't really unexpected given the time of year. This chance to look outside of the country we all knew well was.... It was a one off, too great and opportunity. The profit if we pulled it off was too big, none of us, especially him, ever considered all the options. Too flaming greedy!

He sighed a huge, wind-full sound.

'It might not have been so bad but my Granddad got others into his dream. They were other grown men, maybe not as richly experienced and used to the wildness of the Kimberley as him', he scanned the room, 'but all old enough to make their own choices. When it went wrong the others all blamed him though, suddenly they were gutless. It was then all Granddad's fault, or Dad's, or mine but not theirs. Might have been different with no women allowed in the crew. Someone will remind you, someone might even call you out, I don't know how much the anger lingers up north. But some people reckon they lost a fair slab of what they owned, so it's a fair guess some might remember.'

It was like a pump had drawn the air out of him, his face drooped, his chest sagged, yet we never heard him whimper.

After a pause of perhaps a minute.

'Thanks Dad, but a few more clues might help if you can stand it,' Harry's voice sounded firm, but gentle, comforting, like a parent talking to an errant kid.

'Fair enough call. It's been a long time, more than a lifetime for some, and I haven't dug much of this up for sixty years. Just thought it was only fair to give you a heads up, before you charge into it and get blindsided.'

The sentence was breathless, like Dad hadn't recognised the tone of Harry's question, but felt some urgency to speak its answer.

'For the two previous seasons big wets had pushed storms deep into the desert. Rains had fallen well into what was usually bone dry, red desert country. Everyone knew there must be good pastures out there, but it took Granddad to dare go and have a look. I guess back then the legends of the mighty overland cattle droves of the Duracks still held his and the other pastoralists' minds in that historic vice. Cattle droves were what had started the Kimberley, helping amass our family fortune and many other's fortunes too. Pappy knew courage was associated with risk, just like he knew successfully managing that risk might equal a fortune beyond imagining.'

Looking at Mum he took a last long slow sip, pausing, seemingly to collect scattered memories from where they'd lain for so long they'd become covered in the dust of daily ennui.

'He took four reliable blacks with him, men with strong Aboriginal lore of the dreamtime out that way, all Men who knew all the ancient song-lines, Men who knew the country and all the secret waters, and a young gin. He took minimal hard tucker, expecting we would live hard off the land and its abundant wildlife. As it was we spent nearly a month out, well beyond what later became the Canning Stock route. These days you could do the whole trip in a couple of days with a chopper, but this was then ....'

His tiredness ended with no full stop, just a vacant stare into some past only he could see.

We all waited, Harry spoke.

'But they never took on a huge mob, they mainly just risked their lives and a couple of mounts, didn't they? ' innocently.

'True five hundred head was not a king's ransom back then and just the three men and a pack horse each, some dogs, a couple of guns and that lass, and we thought we 'd taken a wagon load of bush sense.'

He got up and walked slowly back to the cabinet again. 'Want one?' he asked of anyone.

My Harry shook his head.

We all noticed the size he poured.

Dad never had more than one.

'It was what Pappy did when we made it back that started it, the telegram messages he sent to three of the big families' calling them to meet again on Bogabrri. To get them on side originally he'd showed them samples of the grasses he'd cut, told them of vast spans of spaces covered in good grazing, of waterholes lagoons, flocks of wild birds, emu and kangaroo as far as you could ride in a week,' his voice faltering, 'but only a hundred head walked back, the rest left out there. The loss of a few blacks, one a slip of a girl, a lubra at that, worried none of them. They just wanted to know what had happened to lose almost the entire mob, though between them they owned only a couple of hundred. The rest were ours!'

It was obviously still acutely painful from the way his voice had reduced to a whisper.

Into the long silence Gran spoke in her gentle voice, no edge, just what we all knew would be soft honesty, if her head was working properly.

'Everyone can hear the wind howling outside,' and listened intently, her head cocked to one side. 'This winter has rushed us and not one of us has been ready for the aching cold, the sleeting rain or the ferocity of these early winds,' she looked around carefully at each one of us. 'It was like that. No one foresaw it, no one guessed it right, or thought such a big storm would arrive so late in the year. Back then no one had a hundred years of weather records to look up and no one ever thought to ask the old blackfellas, who might have been able to predict it. But no one else could've or did. Even our Cyclone Rosita a few years ago was possibly small by comparison, Rosita blew clear across to Balgo Mission, seven hundred kilometers inland, the rains she left caused immense floods. Way back then no one was in the desert with a rain gauge to measure and record the floods Granddad's mob was hit by, anyway he wasn't the only one to lose everything.'

The way her voice tapered off to nothingness and the sly glance she gave Dad should have alerted me, but I was listening for Dad's story, forgetting Gran was there. Her searching look around the room confirmed we were all listening, but she backtracked to emphasise her point. 'I suspect even Rosita was small by comparison to the one Granddad and his mob shook hands with, out in the Great Sandy Desert in the 1850's. The flooding, the millions of acres that went under water for months, it was too much. Most of the stock perished where they stood, a couple of good stockmen died, and that sweet black girl. All but a couple of horses bolted, never to be seen again.'

She took a deep breath before she finished, 'No cameras to record it, just honesty if you believed them!'

Except for the rattle of a loose sheet of tin on the porch roof, the room was momentarily silent. Gran's face now become ashen, her neck blushed red, her face become ghostly white.'Yet everyone blamed your Great Granddad, that's what the Kimberley weather does to some people on both land and on sea!' her rusty old voice quavered.

Gabby squatted, in tears at the unfairness of the historic prospect Gran had painted.

'As wheat cockies you know the vagaries of weather well enough. Pastoralists and pearlers up north, nearly a hundred years ago, they didn't. Life could be hard as butter back then, licorice like black salty rock.' We all heard the horrid tiredness and confusion that crept back inside her head. I foolishly thought the sudden diversions to pearlers and the sea was some loose figment of her mind.

We turned to look at Dad who'd stood and moved, standing next to Gran's chair and holding her lumpy old hand, towering over her. 'You didn't need to Mum.' ' Nor did you son, it was others who made the mistakes long, long ago but the repercussions of that one storm are still with us. If I can, I might join you in a wee dram.'

She sighed looking guiltily toward the gold liquor in the decanter.

Almost dragging his Ugg-booted feet Dad shuffled to the diminishing Scotch supply. 'Anyone else for a shot, or as Gran more correctly put it, a wee dram?'

Mum stood and walked to the kitchen, where the kettle had been singing, ignored by everyone. In another moment of sudden silence we heard the tea pot emptied of its tired leaf, then the scrape of the tea canister lid.

Two minutes later she appeared, a tray laden with cold buttered gob stuffers, a milk jug and empty cups for all. 'Maybe time for both a less dangerous drink and a less troubled conversation!' We all agreed though Dad continued to give Gran her wee dram. We all watched her inhale a long breath, a draught of the rich perfume of the excellent single malt. 'Ahch, an Auchentoshan isn't it?' she sighed in her imitation Scottish accent, taking a small sip as colour came back to her cheeks. 'The only single I really like. Thanks son you know I can't bear those peaty ones your Dad liked. Taste like they smell. Dank, dirty and slightly rotten, like an old backs camp.'

I found it amazing which bits of her past she remembered, and how in a minute she joined those long ago moments: years apart.

Harry sat mute, but unlike the rest of us had more need than we did for answers.

'Is that why Great Aunt Elizabeth lost the plot?'

'She and Great Aunt Mary never really got over it, the shame, the loss of money and with it loss of status, too hard to cope with at their age and the way they'd been brung up' was Dad's flat response.

'So what was it all for?' Sis asked childishly,' did anything good come from it?'

Gran turned and smiled down at her weakly, 'What good comes from so many things. We all just tried our best. Each of us have had to put up with our individual consequences.' Exhaling a sigh into the cut crystal shot glass.

From the kitchen where she had retired to fill the kettle Mum interjected.

'Everyone remembers that period in the Kimberley best by what was written in 'Kings in Grass Castles' and that's probably for the better.'

Dinner when it came was scraps of food and little talk. I mistakenly thought most of the conversation had been said one way or the other.

Even late the next morning fog held the sheds and paddocks in its damp grey grip, the thick wet air sucked the sounds out of your mouth before your thoughts could crystallize. I'd slept poorly wondering what the true story was.

I'd long been used to going outside when the heavy fogs rolled in, to stand alone, a hundred metres away from the house, and scream. No one had ever heard me, I made sure they were all inside when I exploded.

I'd become used to having the clean feeling inside after a couple of good screams. This time Dad appeared out of the mist from behind me, unseen and unheard and grabbed my shoulder.

The shock of his huge grip cut my scream off like a pair of dress-makers heavy scissors cutting thick fabric.

'What's wrong?' he yelled into my face.

I didn't know how to answer.

It was something I did when the big fogs rolled in.

It didn't mean anything.

I liked the feeling it gave and the cleanness I got inside.

I needed to clean out the feelings built up since Harry said he was going.

The immense sense of privacy the fogs brought with them was a bonus.

'Nothing?' in a child's voice, knowing as I said it that wasn't the answer he needed.

'I just like to come into the fog and scream no one can hear me and it feels good!'

'Christ there are times I worry about you,' and stormed back into the house.

I stood there for ages, not wanting to go inside to be cross-examined. Even Gran wouldn't be on my side, so I stayed buried in the fog until lunchtime.

No one appeared.

Eventually I disappeared down the back of the woolshed to scream again, behind its shelter.

Don't ask me why. I just wanted to do it and see if anyone appeared.

No one did, I strolled back out of the fog just in time for the finale.

But this time as I crept down the hall I knew there was a reason that I felt like screaming. My Harry going north was going to tear a hole in my soul. I knew he needed to and I knew no one else understood that.

Momentarily I wondered if he'd ever gone out and just screamed?

–

Up early, Mum had a 'Traveler,' made. We'd always called food for the road a 'Traveler'. To be sure he didn't starve Harry was cram fed a double ration of eggs, plus ham sliced straight off the bone. By seven a very full Harry was packed, standing on the front-step to say goodbye to the assembled family. Only Gran was missing, but she'd taken Harry aside before being herded off to bed, so presumably her goodbyes had been given.

Harry took Dad's hand in both of his and shook it long and firmly. 'Thanks

Dad, I'll try to keep the family's good name as clean as Kimberley history allows.'

My seldom huggy Dad leant in and hugged his only son, hard.

'You'll do us proud whatever you do son.' then stepped out of my line of sight, taking his dampening eyes out of view.

Mum had kept back to be last, but suddenly wraith-like Gran slipped in next to her, so it was Gran next.

Harry hugged her gently, 'Hang around till I come home Gran, I want to tell you my story, then maybe you can explain the bits of yours we don't know.'

Gran cracked a lopsided grin rather than smile, 'Unless you take a very long time don't worry, anyway you might find the answers by yourself,' and hugged him, with her eyes watering again.

I pushed Sis up, 'You keep growing up Smudge, I want you to be able to lean on me when I see you next,' hugging her till her breath came in gasps.

I was still not ready, but Mum refused to step forward.

'OK it's us then,' my most favourite person muttered, 'No tears, they're for later, you know the answer is yes whatever the question is. Just keep your chin up Fudge.' and his back was disappearing down the steps, to where Mum had retreated.

What they said I never heard but I saw Mum press something into his hand, which he stuffed into his pocket without looking. His hand empty, they hugged for the longest time, before she gave him a motherly shove. He turned on his heel and climbed into his Commodore ute, without looking back.

He was in such a hurry, or perhaps he was crying too, anyway he didn't realise Sis and I had spent the night polishing it in the dry inside the shed, until it glistened.

A lumpy set of brown mud tracks marked his exit through the thick fog out to the front bridge and into the rain, which had begun to crystalise out of the fog.

It soon destroyed our night's hard work.

His shattered dirt tracks blurred, remaining as markers of how we all felt inside.

***

We three kids had shared adjoining rooms along one wing of the house, Harry's room next to mine, Sis on my other side.

Harry was always both physically and personally much closer to me than to Sis. Maybe it was our bedrooms, or maybe just the way we both saw the world. Harry and I would spend as many hours as possible working or playing together, while Sis sat and read alone. To ensure we could chat at night Harry had rigged up a tin-can phone which meant Telstra wouldn't get rich on our long talks.

To connect our bedrooms he'd drilled a large hole in the wall so from my top bunk to his ground level bunk, the string 'phone line' could stretch tight without touching anything. Whenever the string was let to sag or touch something, our 'signal' deteriorated.

It was left to sag after he drove off.

Straight after the sound of his ute faded I'd gone immediately into my Harry's room before the smell of him melded into the woodwork, before the steady rain began to obliterate his shattered tracks. I'd straight away seen Edward T Bear sitting proudly on top of a pile of pillows and thought Harry must have decided it wasn't the sort of thing a bloke should be seen with, so he'd just left him.

You can hardly imagine how glad I was to grab his single remaining scrappy yellow furry ear and hug him to my face. He actually smelt of Harry. Edward T was Harry's oldest toy, the only thing he took to bed each night. The T stood for Teddy, but he was never called Teddy, that would have been childish.

Edward came to live in my room and share my bed, small compensation for the lost phone and the now useless hole. He listened as well as my Harry but never gave advice, unless I gave it to myself pretending my Harry had said it.

Sis got a bit upset when she saw I had him, so to keep peace, and to try to bond with us, I decided she could take him to bed every second night, unless I really needed him and visa-versa.

***

It arrived two days after he left.

A crappy, crumpled envelope, stuck-up with sticky-tape, post marked Perth GPO, inside a scrap of paper torn off some Post- office form. Mum must have seen it but never asked as she sorted the mail collected from our milk-churn letter box, and I never told her. Fortunately some of my mates send weird letters in envelopes stuck together with sticky tape.

I opened it in my room.

G'day fudge, sorry to camoflage the envelop didn't want oldys to recognise my riting and start askin you queschuns. Got a bloke in the post office to adres it lookd at me funny, but so. Don't ask you kno youv always got it.

Yor Harry

A week later a second letter. The other half of the sheet Harry's first missive was torn from, envelope post-marked Manjimup a hundred k's the other way from where he was supposed to be heading.

Hi fudge, Cant belive I'm writin so soon agen went down to perth first yep perth went down not up. remember Alysha from belgum congo that exchange student whose parents came out. well I've been calling her wheneva I was in town we rekon we might be in love so im goin down to manji to pik her up an shes comin north with me. Don't tell oldys!

Ill rite as we go an keep you in tuch im not goin to wor'ry about spellin you can read it an Mum wont mark it. You have know idea how difrent I feel alredy soon as I got out the gate I started to notis change. drivin out from Manji tonite then mite spend a day in perth agen bfore we hed north. If you rite send it to post offis derby that will be next stop. I am so hapy so very hapy it was rite thing to do.

Hope your well cuddl edward I left him for you on my pillo.

Don't ask you kno

Yor harry

CHAPTER FOUR

Sis and gearboxes

A week after Harry left Sis came into my room after dinner noticeably upset all through dinner not talking to anyone so one by one each of us gave up and talked across her.

'Come and give me a cuddle,' from where I lay on my bed-sheet.

'What am I supposed to think everyone says they miss Harry but you all have someone else to talk to Mum has Dad you have Mum and Gran and I have ... that's right...'

Sitting uncomfortably on my doona, long brown legs curled under.

Amy and Eliza are both away for two weeks and I'm not talking to Abby so it's the bike and me tears almost up to her waterline. I let her mumble herself dry, before I arranged to go riding on the next Saturday. 'We both need a day out on the tracks. Let's cut through the far, off the main tracks. I need the smell of cold air in my nostrils to blow a few greyer cobwebs out and you and I need to become better mates.'

Just three years younger there were times the gap might have been a century, except when doing paddock work together. Born a natural stockman on bike or horse, she liked to show off her skills.

***

The day after I offered she shuffled in. Her world looked different.

'Abby rang and apologised, couldn't stand the silence. We both cried, she's coming over, didn't know Harry'd left.'

I knew Abby'd rung, helping Mum chop veggies for dinner, the phone was on the hallstand just a metre away. I didn't let on I'd heard all one end and could guess at the other.

'Wonderful, knew you two would sort it. You always do, she's such a good mate'.

It was easy to smile as I went on. 'I guess that means you want to borrow the Yammy and leave me here while you hoon around with her on a bike that's as good as her Honda. Be careful when you drop the clutch, I've adjusted the throttle, got more of a tendency to buck now'

She was heading down the hall as I finished, Abby would be dropped off by her Mum or Dad with her bike, to stay the weekend. That was cool, I wanted time alone which I wouldn't have with Sis stuck at home alone. I needed to come to grips with the silence in my head and the sudden lack of energy which washed over the place. Sis didn't feel it because she had for so long mostly lived in a world of her own, only coming up for oxygen at meal times.

Mum had become deadly quiet Dad, spending extra time in the shed, going over the equipment ,or sulking. Since her talk to Harry, Gran appeared to have taken a long cruise to lala land. When I asked Mum,' Don't worry' was all I got.

***

The remnants of Dad's once huge family mob have pretty well become city folk and keep to themselves. The only ones we keep in touch with live 60 kms from Melbourne at Mt Macedon, on an amazing garden property, with a beautiful hundred year old, two hectare garden, full of rhododendrons and European trees each over a hundred years old. Dad's brother, who I call Papa, is a retired agricultural scientist, married to Auntie Jenni, an ex-lawyer who used to manage her own small law firm, before they retired to garden. Every few years they fly over to stay and check that Dad's looking after what is still partly their asset. I really like them both.

So a phone call from them wasn't a complete surprise. Mum and Auntie Jenni are good mates, chatting for hours since I hooked up Skype and it doesn't cost to gas on. Mum slipped the headphones on so she could keep working, so I could only hear one end of their chat, filling in gaps by guessing.

Dad lumbered in late dirty and grumpy fingernails filled with black grease, one knuckle bleeding badly. 'Let me clean that up before it gets infected,' Mum scolded, 'you did a good job on it, what were you doing?' as he winced with the application of kettle-hot, soapy water to shift the grease.

'Bloody transfer case, needed to break it open to check why it kept jumping out of range all last harvest. Harry was going to help, he's smarter about gear boxes than me, would almost certainly have known a better way to open the case, but he's gone.' I heard the gap coming, 'unless I want to pay someone, I need to sort it myself.'

'Just hold still', Mum growled, 'I'll need to snip off that flap of loose skin. I think it's too dirty to bother with a proper stitch. You just have to keep an Elastoplast on for a week, then I'll have another look.'

I got up from where I'd been studying to put my two bobs worth in.

'Couldn't help overhearing Dad, would you like me to give you a hand?' I asked timidly, looking with interest at the great flap of detached oil encrusted skin Mum had placed on the bench.

I used it to ease in further.

'Not a bad piece. If it was a bit bigger I could tan it and make one side of a wallet.'

Mum shushed me Dad grinned.

I was part way in, 'I don't think you'd be much good inside the Header gear transfer box Fudge' he stated flatly, with a fake flaky smile. I smiled my own fake sweet little daughter smile loudly, right back at him.

'Well maybe not but I could find a blown-up diagram on the web and check what the manual said. I waited a few seconds, or do you still have the old manual?' knowing full well he didn't, because Harry'd searched everywhere before, then had me go on-line to look it up during harvest and explained it that night. Harry was planning on still being here to fix it, he didn't but I knew how he was going to crack the case and what he intended to do to fix the probable cause.

That got Dad's full attention, 'I'll print up an exploded view and see it we can work it out together'. He very careful to emphasise the we and together, neglecting the Harry. I knew my Harry would be pleased when I fixed the problem.

Next morning I spent an hour with Dad taking the top of the box off, almost too quickly spotting the broken part of a slip ring, which the blog I printed for

Dad's sake said was the common cause of the same problem all over the country.

It didn't change his view instantly. But after I helped him crack open and pull that great lump of a gearbox apart and by the time I'd shown him how to slide the transfer box both in and out under another shaft I thought I had him.

Inside early for morning tea, the job was done and with a grin right across his smiling, unshaven, whiskery face, Mum looked up surprised as we banged the screen door coming in.

'I haven't got a batch of scones on yet, no idea you'd be in so early. Do you have to go into town for a spare part? I need a few things?'

Dad's next line I loved so much that that night as I lay in bed reviewing the day I scratched it onto my memory tree. 'Well we would have but Fudge blogged it or something and somehow she also knew Case didn't have one in town, but the same part was used in the Fergy 65. She knew we just happened to have an old Fergie box off the one I retired a couple of years ago, the one I'm keeping to use for spares for the new Fergie, no idea they had interchangeable parts. Smart kid this girl of ours.'

You could have scrapped my smile off the kitchen table.

Morning tea slid easily into a pleasant discussion which I directed about my going away to High school and how I could still help from wherever I was because of my skills web searching and blogging never giving a hint of Harry's involvement.

He did not want to farm. He'd left home, and I was still here working on Dad. Softly, softly, catchee monkey.

Harry had barely stepped off the ladder and I'd managed to get one foot on it.

CHAPTER FIVE

Our dogs and stuff

It was never just me who thought Poppa was the best dog breeder and trainer in the world. Harry did too, plus heaps of neighbors have our pups even Dad grudgingly gives him that accolade. Old Buster, his last top dog, was so clever he could nearly count sheep through gates, actually sex ewes from rams when mating was finished and easily separate lambs from their mothers. Around here lots want Buster to breed with their bitches. Poppa's used him to help me train Bop.

Bop came from a litter from Dad's top dog Boozer, a red-cloud Kelpie, with Poppa's oldest bitch Renee, a black and tan kelpie. In his day Boozer was said to be an awesome paddock worker in her hey-day Renee could thread sheep through a needle run over their backs in the yards and pack them perfectly in pens inside the shed. Breeding dogs with both paddock and yard-skills was a sure way to predict pups from their blending should be great, the final result down to whoever trained them.

Bop's on the small-side what they call the 'runt' from a litter-of eight squirming black and white balls. In big litters there's one smaller than its siblings so it gets last suck at feeding time.

That was Bop.

Runts almost never get a full feed off the teat so never grow to their potential size though their brains seem fine. Poppa joked he must have been a runt as he was so small while his brothers were larger.

Poppa reckons runts are always good dogs.

'We runts learn to look out for ourselves working tricky ways to get what we want whenever bigger siblings push in our way, carries over when we're older and need to work stuff out' Poppa crowed.

Bops' two years old, trained every day, sometimes twice, up to an hour a time. No one's going to say I never taught her to reach full potential. She comes to whistle or call, drops and sits on command, whatever distractions are happening, no matter how close or far away she is. She's taking a bit too long to learn to stay put until I tell her 'free', Poppa reckons that's Boozers 'fault line'. He never sat as long as he should have.

Both are essential skills in a working dog, like the skill to creep up to a sheep instead of spooking them, something Bop has naturally and I've worked to refine.

Poppa got cranky when he spotted me throwing a ball for Bop, almost yelling in his frustration. 'If you want a ball chaser go ahead. If you want a working dog just train her properly and cut out the games.'

To her frustration Bop never played ball again but found balls everywhere, fetched them and dropped them at my feet only to look disappointed when I pocketed them.

Her genealogy comes from a long line of working dogs on both sides, some paddock legends, some great yard dogs. None were known as tennis-ball dogs.

Poppa said with her breeding she wouldn't need much training just to be shown when to do the things she already knew in her head. He believes working skills are transmitted genetically. If that's true it's pretty important to make sure matings bring together the best of both gene pools.

Training a dog to sit and wait while stock settle or move on is a critical talent. Sometimes you need to let stock calm down to make sure they don't crush as they go through a gate. It's proving hard to teach Bop, she just wants to go, go, go.

Too much force has come though from Boozer he always was hard to steady up, was Pop's only comment when he saw her failing to steady up.

***

By the time I knew him Buster was fully grown living his whole life on Walkaway.

He knew every square centimeter and was smart enough to remember every difficult sheep and problem bull. He was getting slow so we didn't use him any more than we had to. He rode everywhere in the back of the ute and spoke up when told to. Like Poppa his hips were giving him gyp but he was stoic and not showing any pain as keen as mustard to jump out of the ute and show off whenever he could but needing a hand-up to get back in.

His pain stopped suddenly a year back not long before Poppa passed away. A hot day during crutching Buster would not stay out of the yards. Late in a long day I noticed he'd ceased barking down the back when I told him to speak up. Too busy to check I managed without him. A fair bit later when checking the gates I found him curled up next to the rear fence looking as if he'd just paused for a bit of a breather.

Poppa was terribly upset. Picking him up gently in his arms he carried him to the ute before asking me to dig a decent hole. Out under the big Candlebark back behind the yards, that way his ghost can duck in for a look whenever we're working a mob. He'd like that.

***

We didn't do another shearing before Poppa died and I lost my best mate, mentor and dog handler.

***

Bop's always on my heels when I'm home and always tied up if I'm at school, never allowed to just roam the farm no more than Renee and Boozer or Buster were. It's one of the rules on our farm that all dogs are tied up when they're not working or under control of their owner. Along the same line is the rule that only a dog's owner can feed it so a dog always knows who's the boss-dog. Dad goes a bit further and uses a rule he learnt as a jackeroo in the Riverina. Only a dog's owner can pat it so only he can pat Renee and Boozer. Poppa was relaxed about that rule so I could pat Buster but not play games or feed him.

***

My best friend Yonke has no working dog; she has a big jet-black Spaniel called Boudewijn which in Dutch means 'brave friend'. Pronounced Boodwin she calls him Boodi except when he's in trouble. Because he's not trained he never comes to our place and Bop never goes to hers, but after weekends together they know the other's scent so can tell where we've been.

Boodi has heaps of bad habits. Being allowed to run free he nicks off and goes everywhere whether Yonke is home or away. When she's home he tends to stay around the house. At night he chases possums foxes and roos dragging his catch home to drop outside the kitchen door as if asking for them to be cooked.

Yonke has to dispose of the mangled half eaten carcasses.

Poppa told her she'd ruined a good hunter but it was too late to retrain him. She told him she didn't care Boodi was a free spirit and should not have been trained to be tied up. I looked away.

***

While there are always heaps of interesting jobs to be done, school gets in the way a fair bit. It's not like I don't get to do many jobs at seeding or harvesting time but not those needing machinery which is maybe just as well as they both mean driving giant machines that I can't really handle properly yet. In a normal year both periods arrive during school holidays then if I'm around, I get to sit in the cabin with Dad handling the wheel or using the other controls as I learn to drive both.

I enjoy stock work more than machines stuff while on the other hand Dad would rather do any job with a machine than work with stock. In the sheep yards you regularly hear him going off. Dumb animal, a machine does what you make it do, bloody sheep don't have much in the way of brains so no when they try to think it's total bloody confusion, and so on often blunter than that.

He tried to explain that view one day after a sheep had beaten him in a battle of wits as he tried getting a small mob into the yards I grinned. Thank goodness we've got good sheep dogs Dad. They don't get as cranky as you do; they just try again until the mob finally gets the idea of where they're supposed to go.

A scowl was his response.

CHAPTER SIX

With Harry gone

With no Harry to help and me about to leave for High-school Dad was forced to recognise the farm required a new station hand. He'd raised it with Mum over morning tea after a morning struggling to fix another part on the header, sending me to the computer to find a remedy.

How do you reckon we should go about getting a decent station hand? Bert's getting beyond it. If he gets any skinnier I'll lose sight of him when he stands still or walks into the scrub on a cloudy day. There are supposed to be thousands of unemployed lads around collecting the dole. There must be one who'll suit us. I can slowly retire Bert and just keep him on the payroll. He should be getting the pension by now you might need to assist in that department.

I suggested Dad put an ad in the Weekly but instead he got Mum to contact Centrelink which I didn't know he knew existed let alone who they were or what they did.

Surprises sometimes Dad's full of them.

***

Bert was about eighty no one knew for sure and he wasn't giving the secret to any scrawny girl, daughter of the boss or not no matter how often I asked. He'd been on Walkaway so long no-one admitted remembering when he came or where he'd come from.

Except for a few weeks around Melbourne cup time he was utterly reliable, but the first Tuesday in November would always find him in Melbourne visiting his sister. She conveniently lived in Flemington a short walk from the famous racecourse where they run one of the most famous distance races in the world.

Each year a couple of days before the big race Bert took his holidays and headed down via the bus.

Harry was pumping him about the race carnival when he discovered Bert first went shopping for a new set of 'duds' and also found out Bert had a girlfriend. The girlfriend was an ex-madam who'd allegedly once owned a house of ill repute but was now a respectable lady.

Lucy's entertained me each trip since I met her the first time I went down.

Harry never found out what 'entertained' meant and I doubt they did anything that could not be retold to an archbishop over cream and warm scones. Certainly when he spilled the beans he never gave Harry any indication of hanky-panky and in his later years even thinking about it would have killed him.

She accompanied him to the race carnival and about town for two weeks.

She lives with me. We shack up in the flashest hotel in Melbourne, drink champagne with breakfast and eat oysters and canapés, he bragged to Harry. Such a diet must have wreaked havoc on the stomach of a man who otherwise spent all year eating cold spam sandwiches between slices of even colder hard toast, with a stubby of 4X beer to wash it down.

Champagne is what you drink during the Cup an' a pretty lady on your arm is important. A man has to shave twice a day though, he told Harry when pressed for details.

We noticed Bert's memories of the races were becoming fuzzy. Where once he could recount the entire fields and both winners and place getters going back years through some trick of his mind only the really early Cups remained memorable.

His annual trip ceased after he got a letter from his sister telling him Lucy had passed on.

He seldom had to read anything or receive a letter. I don't think anyone except Dad knew he was illiterate. Like so many of his generation in the bush Bert only attended primary school for a couple of early years where he learnt his numbers well enough to pass muster with keeping paddock counts but that was it.

We only get mail delivery twice a week and this was the Tuesday mail day. I was giving a hand and had excised the pale pink envelope from our mess of bills and flyers before I noticed who it was to. I decided to walk it down to his hut just for a bit of exercise and was surprised to see Bert leaning on the rail as I walked out of the office.

In his slow, laconic fly excluding drawl he asked politely.

'Any chance there might be a letter for me t'day?' he wheezed a soggy rollie hanging limp between his dark brown nicotine stained fingers after spending its morning dropping between his lips.

Even to see Bert outside the office was a surprise but for him to ask about mail almost confounded me. I paused not to withhold the letter but in response to the small shock. Had a feeling in my bones there might be something about Missus smiling his stained gappy-tooth grin. Not exactly the same but similar to the one displayed when he left his top plate false teeth out by mistake.

I passed him the pink letter, feeling the thick calloused skin on his blunt finger tips as we accidentally brushed hands. Squatting on the porch of the homestead he tore it open carefully teased out the single page smelt it seemed to read it and only then asked. 'Any chance you might read it for a chap, havn't got my reading glasses on.'

I smiled my yes, noticing his usually gentle, sunburned wrinkles which so easily creased into smiles were unusually tight.

Plainly it was bad news.

I asked if he knew who it was from.

'That's my sister's perfume so it'll be bad news. Had the feeling in me bones it was coming.'

His sister's handwriting was simple old-fashioned penmanship from when kids learned to write in school. Not many capitals though. The single sheet of paper was pale pink with a border of flowers around each side, not exactly happy but not funereal either.

Dear Bert,

Hoped I'd never have to write this letter. I hoped I might go first. Lucy didn't turn up for our weekly lunch at the corner café. She hadn't rung to confirm but last time she was fine so I walked round to her place in Fletcher St.

Arrived just as the ambulance pulled up. Let them in with my key.

Lucy looked like she'd just dozed off. Smile on her face, lippy on and her usual touch of blush. Must've got dressed and lay down for a nanna nap. Had on that nice pink floral dress she wore to the races last year, the one you really liked.

Ambulance fellow checked said she'd been gone an hour or so. Looks like it was peaceful no sign of a struggle or distress.

Lucky when it's like that, they took her away.

I straight away thought about you, thought of phoning but reckoned I might cry a letter was better. You can look at it later, not like a phone call.

Never a good enough thing to say when someone as special as Lucy dies.

Always wished you two had tied the knot and so did Lucy but I guess you were a bit set in your ways by the time she came along.

Funeral was yesterday in the City cemetery. Big heap of flowers must have had lots of happy customers over the year but none turned up.

Knew you don't like funerals so never got in touch.

Just me, her friend Mabel and the two next-door neighbors, those blessed sticky beaks. Never spoke to them, knew Lucy didn't like them, but they was the ones as rang the ambulance. Must've known her habits.

Mabel and me lashed out on a taxi back to Lucy's house, she offered to pay but I insisted. Sat and had a cuppa, out of that fancy tea pot Lucy liked to fetch out on special occasions. We both reckoned it was a special occasion and all that, so she wouldn't mind, might even have been happy Mable reckoned. Big house as you know, but neat as a pin, like maybe she was expecting company. She had a bit of that three-coloured sponge in the fridge too. We had a bite and Mabel took the rest home for her grandkids, shame to waste it.

I'll pack all her stuff up, so if there is something you might like to keep just ask, otherwise it will all go to the Good Sami's. Lots of nice photos of her and you if you want one. You'll remember there's no kids. Figure I might find a Will as I tidy up. Feels strange with her not in the house,

Love,
your little sister Dot.

As I turned to hug him I spotted a thin dribble of tears running down his dusty dry old cheeks. Mum wasn't home, it was up to me so I headed toward the homestead, come inside for a cuppa Bert, I reckon we both might need one.

I'd heard Mum say it to a dozen people over the years. No fuss, just a friendly invite.

'Wouldn't mind one if you could. Sort of knocks a bloke about news like that.'

As we walked across the porch to the kitchen door he took his sweat-stained, probably once fawn hat off. In all the years I had known Bert I'd never seen his bald head before, to me it was like the hat and Bert were welded together. I think I'd imagined he even wore it to bed.

But he knew his manners.

I don't know why but I got Mum's best Royal Albert tea-set out. Maybe it was me showing I knew my manners too, maybe it was something else. He stood uncertainly, until I told him to sit, pointing to Dad's big chair, the one with the arms. I thought it would make him feel more comfortable but he looked strange sitting there in Dad's chair, his greasy grey scalp with a few wisps of surprisingly black hair stuck across his grayish skull.

While the kettle was coming to the boil I got out some cold scones, a pat of butter and some cream. I caught him looking at me as I sniffed it. 'Not sure if its fresh', I apologised. 'Always smell mine too even if it's straight from the old Bessie just a sensible habit', he smiled back.

I passed him a cup of blackest tea like I knew he liked in the paddock when I took smoko out to Dad and him.

'Hope the tea is strong enough. I know you like it pretty black?'

'Looks grouse,' he grinned his big gentle grin, 'Always figured folk prob'ly make it weak in good china but not you. Make a chap a good missus one day!'

'One day I might even own a set like this so I can play the lady. For now I'll just use Mum's best', feeling nice inside he'd even noticed.

***

The tension was not there like I'd expected, but still I tested the waters gently.

'Sounds like Lucy was pretty special. Your sister must have been a good mate and liked her a lot? '

He looked up from staring down at the tablecloth.

'Dot liked her a lot. Like she said reckoned we should've got hitched. But Lucy'd had a decent hubby before so I reckoned I might be a bit too rough. Just couldn't see Lucy living out here and the city's not for me 'cept for the carnival fortnight.'

He smiled broadly as he sat across from me in his crisply ironed, bold check, work shirt.

I reckoned he might have been wrong.

'So race time was a special time for you both. Parties, champagne and caviar Harry said?'

Bert's tired old face cracked along well practiced smile lines.

'Kept me going with memories, all year, Golly we used to kick our heels up something terrible. Once had to be bailed out some bloke was coming on to her and I snotted him one. Good square hit right on his button. Cops let me out after the bloke went home and said it was fair enough what I done. Never even got a record but he got a busted nose to remind him to be more polite. Lucy said her hubby would've been proud of me, if he'd been around,' and smiled easily at the memory.

An instant image came of Bert scrubbed up in his city duds, streaks of black hair slicked back with Brylcream shiny shoes, a not too loud tie correctly knotted and Lucy beside him in a pink floral dress instantly falling in love with her champion. The other bloke must have got a helluva shock when Bert hauled back and laid one on him. There isn't a lot of Bert, but I imagine he was handy with his fists. Just a consequence of growing up in the bush.

'So did you go partying after they let you out? I grinned at this old man, now slid deep in his memories.

'We did that, finished up at the pub on the corner of Flinders St opposite the railway station. Place called Young and Jacksons. Went upstairs and had a peek at that Chloe painting as well. I told Lucy I thought she was a cut above Chloe. Said she wanted to walk, held my hand all the way home wouldn't let me get a cab, though its miles away. Lucky I'm used to walkin out here, 'n Lucy kept up pretty easy,' and he paused to look at me, 'but you're maybe a bit young for talkin about that kind of stuff.

I took my cue and headed the conversation away from Melbourne and drove it up north, taking a couple of big guesses, trying to make it seem I knew more than I did.

'So how bad was the big blow that took most of the mob, was Poppa hurt?'

He never winced, just followed my lead. I could possibly have asked him anything he just needed to talk.

'Amazing chap your Granddad, would've followed him anywhere, the camp blacks would've too. But liked the bottle a bit he did, that was maybe part of it. No-one saw the weather until the river got up. Had rained way out to the south east more used to storms comin from the north. Might've mattered if we did see it somewhere to run to or pick a better camp. Water spooked the mob winds blew the canvases away in minutes then days of rain; so heavy couldn't see your hand in front of your face. Blew and rained like that for two days. When we turned out to get what few stock was left practically none was found. Stock had took fright 'n bolted into the wide blue. A full blown river appeared out of nowhere one poor black dragged me out of it. Never even knew his name, but I saw him swept away, creek too fast, and I couldn't swim but got lucky. Others just hid wherever they could. That poor girl just got trampled by the mob.

Ammo was powder, so shot and ball went to mush, guns made useless. Last few horses was badly spooked so we headed for home. Cattle nowhere to be seen, even on spaces as wide as those plains were. Must've bolted clear up to Darwin, or drowned. Just scooped up the few poor blighters we spotted, all spooked, so was easy to bring into a mob, reken they was glad of some company.'

He stopped, deep in memory, 'Another cuppa might keep the mind ticking over!'

'So when the locals all went feral you came south with Dad?' I asked over my shoulder while refilling the pot from the kettle still bubbling away on the AGA, speaking as if I knew the answer.

'No point even talking to them. Gutless mob none of the vision like your Granddad had. It sent him near broke. This place was already here so caught the steamer down. Had to learn to start again, growing grain, no end to what a man can do if he must and we certainly had to after that lot went mongrel.'

After a sip or two of red hot tea with no sugar he looked across directly at me.

'Couldn't stay up there, no stock, no staff, no friends. Not easy to leave for both of us. Your Granddad lost heaps, including his reputation. I decided to went with him, maybe left a few mates.'

He took long pause and stared back into his history before he continued.

'Them other winging buggers just lost a few cows.'

The freshly brewed tea was too hot, so like Gran did he poured the scalding tea into the saucer to cool, then slurped noisily from the edge.

'Probably only made one mistake. Should have married Lucy might've been the making of me. Hubby'd been dead over twenty years.'

His voice sounded tired and wistful his mouth sagging toward the corners.

I looked away.

'From the little I know about life Bert some things like that we only get one chance at. Sounds like you had plenty, just decided it would be too hard for her. I reckon you might have been right. A city girl up here before conveniences came, pretty tough to cope with.'

He drained his saucer and stood, pushing his chair back quietly.

'Thanks for the cuppa char and chat feel better. See you in the paddock,' he murmured his traditional farewell, showing his manners as he went out the back door to walk to his hut, collecting his greasy hat before jamming it back in place.

***

I was sick in bed with a heavy chest cold for the next few days so never came down, eating light meals in bed. The first meal I ate at the dinner table Dad came in early. 'Been talking to Bert you made a pretty good impression on him, said you were a good listener and made a bloody good cuppa sent his regards to get better.'

I kept quiet, not sure what Bert might've told him.

'What did you two find to talk about. Hardly one to have a conversation of more than two words with.'

'Had a letter from his sister and asked me to read it to him. His girlfriend had died. He just wanted some company so I made him a cuppa or two.'

'Told you all about it, did he ?' he probed.

'No just as much as he needed to settle himself a bit,' I parried.

'Fair enough well done he can be a dour old bugger not given to chatting.'

'Like you Dad and I can even get a conversation going with you if I need to!'

'Touche.' offered Mum who'd sat silently on the end of the bed, grinning though it all.

***

I'd messaged Harry while in bed, an outline of the details Bert had passed on about the Kimberley storm. I didn't think he'd want to know about Lucy just then. Late Friday night I woke to the ping I'd been waiting for as Harry's reply came in. I was asleep but got up.

So far so good, staying at a place called El Questro, right up north, Holiday Lodge, totally awesome place, million acres, huge river pools, great motel too, got a job as handyman, Alysha kitchen hand, room provided. XXX bro

I slept well, imagining Harry and Alysha trying to work out a life together and glad he hadn't waited like Bert. I guessed Alysha had helped with the spelling and punctuation like Lucy might have.

***

Saturday I went to town with Mum and Gran, nothing important, just shopping for food and more incontinence nappies for Gran. She hates them but they mean she can stop worrying about when the urge to pee might come. A few weeks back she was grateful she wore them. A stray dog came onto the farm, looking for Dad's bitch which had come on heat. Gran saw it and tried to chase it away with her walking stick. It turned and bit her on the bum! Fortunately she had two pairs of pads on, so it got nothing for its trouble but a good whack. Dad was just driving in and saw it all had the rifle in his hand before the mongrel made it ten metres.

No tag so no one to tell. 'Be one of them bloody town dogs increased in numbers with the mining boom. Those blow in-blow blow-out mining people leave their cats and dogs when they shift towns and we have to clean up their mess.' Dad cursed as he dragged the stiffening carcass away to burn before the crows made a bigger mess of it than his shot had.

***

Apart from our shopping Mum bought a bag of boiled sweets for Bert one of the few treats we knew he actually liked apart from going to the Cup. As you drive back into Walkaway you have to swing past the hut Bert's lived in ever since he came down with Dad. As we drove up it looked spectacular, bold purple Bougainvillea climbing over the front in a vivid profusion of bloom. On what she thought was an impulse Mum decided to just pop in to give the sweets to him instead of waiting until he came to the office on Monday. 'He might enjoy them over the weekend and add a bit of cheer to his otherwise quiet and lonely weekends.'

She was out in a minute, her face ashen.

'He's passed away in the deck chair out the back in the sun,' said in one breathless sentence as she climbed in.

I heard Gran groan and sigh in the front passenger's seat.

I could not believe he could really have died, he'd seemed so OK only a few short hours ago. I reached to open my door to go see for myself.

'Don't go darling he just looks like he went to sleep there's nothing we can do. I'll tell Dad and we can arrange a funeral for him.'

Looking back to the stunning purple display that draped the whole front she pensively added 'I guess we'll be his only mourners?''

'No Mum there's a younger sister in Melbourne who wrote she might want to come. I know her.'

I lied, a little white one.

I wanted to pass the sad news on to someone whose life I'd only recently become aware of and who I wanted to say a goodbye to.

'I know her address. I should be able to find her number and call to tell her. I'll do it I sort of know her after talking to Bert last week.'

***

I went in through the never locked front door.

Inside Bert's hut was a mirror of his life.

A single room with an adjacent bathroom.

Spartan.

A wire framed bed, covered with a creaseless, simple grey, ex-army blanket, a small worn-out, once red mat lay see-through flat on the floor next to it. Alongside his bunk was propped an unpainted, cigarette-burned bedside table, despite the empty tobacco-tin ashtray parked perfectly in the middle.

The simple wooden kitchen table had the one chair pushed in tidily.

A two-door wooden pantry cupboard, with only one door, held a few chipped plates and cups, a packet of tea, a tin of tomato soup and an almost empty box of Weetbix, the flap torn off neatly.

To the inside of the remaining door, stuck on with sticky tape, were two photos of Bert with a very attractive older lady. She was holding his arm, a grandstand full of well dressed punters in the background, had to be Lucy.

Bert was clean shaven, smiling a huge grin, dressed in a fancy three-piece suit, a small checked hat perched rakishly, setting him off as I'd never imagined him.

On the sink, so well scrubbed it had developed a matt-finish stainless steel patina, lounged a large cream coloured, tin tea canister. Keeping it company was propped a bowl, so recently washed it was still drip-drying, accompanied by a desert spoon face down, with a tiny crust of oats near the neck. On the bleach-scrubbed wooden bench a single battered aluminium porridge saucepan lay face down, looking well loved. The round shouldered cream Kelvinator kero fridge stood alone in the corner, oily smoke stains climbing darkly up the wall.

I did think to open the door and check its contents but decided against it.

Declaring all his clothes to the world stood a once two-door wardrobe, with the left hand door long missing. When I said something about it to Dad later he just grinned as he commented flatly.

'Probably decided it was a waste of time opening and shutting the door so took it off, Bert was like that, never saw the point in two words if one would do.'

Inside hung two folded pairs of once-beige Yacka work trousers, two ironed RM

Williams blue check shirts each on its own hanger. Hung alone was a buffed up, twelve-plait dark brown kangaroo leather belt that I knew Bert had shot, skinned tanned and plaited himself.

I momentarily wondered where his flash city clothes were kept.

On the well worn pine floor in front of the robe were propped his good pair of well-worn RM Williams green-hide work boots. The slightly open top drawer bulged with black socks and matching jocks, the drawer beneath doing its duty full of singlets. All dark blue.

The room smelt of Bert, not testosterone sweaty like Harry's, sort of warm and cuddly. The pillow slip was rather grey and greasy like his hair, I knew for sure he took his hat off at night.

Leaning precariously against the end of the wardrobe was a fold-up ironing board. A simple pre-steamer iron, perched on top of the wardrobe, its frayed tattered, multi-coloured cord hanging forlornly across the space left open by the missing door.

Bert had ironed his last work shirt.

Feeling as if I was invading the privacy of his inner sanctuary I took a quick look around.

It sat there on the cigarette singed bedside table, a beat up, indexed, red leather address book, which I rifled through.

His address book, very few names not already crossed out.

I instantly knew Lucy would now have had a line drawn though.

Found Nancy, easily scribbled under 'Dot' and with nothing to copy the number to, I picked it up, starting walking toward the door to go back to the homestead. On an impulse I stepped back and opened his bedside table drawer.

Under a Tilley lamp sitting as if it owned the space it was tidy, neat and clean except for a bundle of bank deposit books, a battered old Bible and a single envelope marked 'Last Will and Testament'.

I picked up both the still creaseless envelope and the leather-bound Bible, more interested in it than the envelope. I'd never imagined Bert having one and now that I knew he couldn't read I was fascinated.

The once leather covered Bible fell open at Psalm 23.

The thin vellum pages were worn, their edges dirty. 'The Lord is my shepherd,

I shall not want ' was as far as I got before I teared up and put it down.

I knew what words I would say over Bert's grave.

I hesitated to walk out the back and actually say my goodbyes, but Aboriginals believe the spirit would be hanging around and can see and hear you, and after so long on Walkaway Bert deserved a goodbye.

As I opened the screen-door to the small north facing back porch the first thing I saw was his hatless head above the back of an unpainted, unstained wooden recliner chair.

His hat lying behind it, upside down on the porch. I stepped out and bent to pick it up, to gently replace it where it would feel right to him. As I looked at that tired, pale skull I wondered when someone last kissed him goodnight, like mum does to me at night. The impulse to kiss him goodnight and goodbye was too strong, so I bent to kiss him for the first and last time.

His hair smelt of shampoo and brylcream his scalp was warm.

At first I thought it must have been from the sun.

'Goodbye old friend, travel well I will miss you until we meet in the yards,' and like

they say in novels, I felt an unbidden a tear drop from my eye.

I stepped away and in one more step was off the small deck.

I looked back as I thought I heard him softly whisper.

'Thanks for the hat and the kiss, see you in the big paddock' he hadn't moved.

It must have been something I dreamt.

I walked slowly back to the homestead, Bert's death making me so aware of the impermanence of life, the need to be nice when you can, and take nothing for granted. I walked in around the back up on the verandah to come into my room via the French doors, forgetting until I was about to step up onto the boards that way took me past the cage.

On an impulse I plucked a couple of thistles going to seed. Both birds loved them. As I pushed one into the wire mesh I looked at Cockyone, 'How r ya mate?' he shrieked, ;It's alright here, been better tho,' something Bert taught him long ago.

'How about you followed Cockytwo,' as I shuffled inside I wondered was Bert playing games with me

***

Nancy was her name. She answered to it as she picked up the phone. 'Nancy: who's that?' in that slightly creaky voice partially deaf old people often have on the phone.

'My name is Kimberley,' I started.

'Oh no don't tell me, just got his letter in the morning mail. He told me all about you. Said you might like Mabel's Royal Albert tea set. Is he all right or has he hurt himself doing something stupid. He's never learned to slow down. He would be eighty one today you know. I still have his card here, meant to post it last week but been a bit off since Lucy went.'

I didn't know but the card could wait.

Bert would never be eighty two.

'Nancy I have awful news!' I started again.

'Oh no! I should never have told him about Lucy. It will have broken his heart, if only, if only, how did he die?'

'Asleep in his favourite sun-chair out the back on his verandah. Mum found him a while ago and I knew about you because I read your letter out to him about Lucy. I found your address and phone in his book.'

She was not listening.

'All he scribbled me back was, little Kimberley wants her tea set.'

I began to cry out loud. He had watched me be careful with Mum's best set and must have scribbled straight away.

Nancy said she would come over, if we could meet her at the airport. It was the least we could do after all her brother had done for us. Mum and I drove in together, arriving just in time to see this sprightly lady, in a pink floral dress, walk steadily down the gangplank, a cardboard box cradled in her arms.

'That'll be Nancy, she's wearing the same dress Bert described, the one Lucy wore to the races. The one she was dressed up in to go to tea with Nancy, the day she passed away.'

'Obviously not superstitious,' Mum muttered as we walked out onto the tarmac to meet her.

Nancy was easy to be with, a bit deaf, but chatty and friendly. The cardboard box held Lucy's tea set: four cups and saucers and a beautiful floral teapot, nicer than Mum's, each piece carefully wrapped in white tissue paper.

'Wrapped it up, careful like. Carried it all the way, didn't let them shove it up top. Saved on post too. Hope it's what you wanted?' was how she described the most perfect and precious gift I could think of to remember Bert by.

She was obviously embarrassed when I gave her a big hug.

'It's so perfect and such a nice thing for you to carry all that way.'

***

She wanted to stay in Bert's hut for her two days with us.

'Rather like to see for myself what Lucy would have had to put up with,' was all she said when Mum tried to cajole her to stay in Harry's room.

All she took back was Bert's grease-rimmed hat, along with the sure knowledge that her brother was right. Lucy would not have liked it enough to stay.

***

Without ceremony we laid Bert to his final rest in Walkaway's tiny cemetery, with its rusty cast-iron fence and that wooden gate we must fix one day. The coffin made of simple pine was carried from the homestead to the cemetery on the back of the battered, paint chipped, unlicensed old Landrover ute, Bert had owned. A mass of Agapanthus was all the flowers I could find, but I carefully picked all the snails off, before I arranged them neatly.

A simple wooden cross, with Bert carved into it, is all that an inquisitive historian will find of a wonderful man and his interesting life. Mum arranged for the local pastor to say a few words. He never said much; he never knew Bert.

I stepped up after him and opened Bert's Bible. I got out the lines 'The Lord is my Shepherd I shall not want, he maketh me to lie down in green pastures he leadeth me beside still waters..' and stopped, that was all Bert would need to be comfortable in the big paddock.

I picked up a handful, with everyone following my example taking turns to cast handfuls of Walkaway's rich red dirt on the dear old man's last resting place.

Dad came over putting his arm around me, ' That was strong Kimberley.'

I looked up at him and threw the dice again. 'I'm not a kid anymore Dad, ask anyone', gave him a hug and walked over to Nancy / Dot.

Later in the day Mum and I drove Nancy into Geraldton airport with plenty of time to spare. She was quite chatty considering.' Very kind of you and your husband hardly said thanks to him. Bert loved him like a father, been with him since your husband was a pup but you know that.'

I didn't and was not sure Mum did from her reply,' Not really. They were both alike few words. Did he write often?

I knew the answer before she spoke.

'Pretty well illiterate never been to past grade three school. Before this last note just one card. He did it in grade two to Mum signed his name sort of. Mum always kept it I've got it now. He just arrived same day each year and stopped over for the Cup carnival didn't stay at home just came by to pick up the last years suit and for a cuppa or two. Bought a new suit every year. I have a wardrobe full of them going back years, a bit of a museum of clothes, about the only thing I ever saw him spend a quid on. He shacked up in some flash pub with Lucy. Lovely lass, you would've liked her, but she wouldn't have liked Walkaway. A city girl you know.'

I understood why there were no flash clothes in the wardrobe.

Wandering off I looked at travel brochures, leaving them chatting at the only table in the otherwise deserted arrivals lounge of Geraldton airport with a plate of biscuits and a tea pot to lubricate their chat.

Nancy gave me a big hug when her flight was called. 'I'll send you a letter when I settle down, really glad Bert had you for a friend. I can see why he was fond of you.'

And she was gone.

***

It was week or two before Mum got around to sorting out the few possessions Bert left, making up a bag for the Good Sami's. Somehow after the funeral his Will had slipped into his old Bible, missed until it fell out weeks later when I was thumbing through, thinking of Bert scanning the pages at night before he dimmed the wick on his Tilley lamp.

He'd left his entire estate to be divided between Harry Sis and me. His Bank book was one of a series with the same Bank, which had changed its name twice during the many years he'd been a customer. The faded blue books went right back to his time in the Kimberley, all held in two bundles with rubber bands. Deposit entry after deposit entry, and apart from the two weeks of Melbourne Cup carnival expenses almost no withdrawals.

Mum always bought his boots strides and the odd shirt in town then debited his pay. Food was provided by the farm and the boxes of Weetbix and jars of jam were from our stores, also deducted before he got his pay. That was the way it had been on the station up north, that was the way Bert liked it, not for him walking down the supermarket isles.

I had to wonder why he worked at all as he had so few pleasures in his life.

Harry Sis and I were suddenly very rich by our standards. Fifty thousand dollars each. Bert's Bank book showed he had not lied. He really had won big at the Cup a few times, then deposited it straight into his bank, in the middle of November.

Not knowing what to do with it I put it into my Bank account promising not to let it finish up like Bert's.

I waited for Harry to ring.

I thought I'd dealt with Bert's death fairly well. Death in animals was common and had my share of rellies who moved on, but two weeks after Lucy flew out I found myself suddenly crying.

I'd jumped into Mum's car to go to Jamiesons to find a tractor part in their shed. Passing our cemetery, because I wasn't looking my mind drifted to Bert and I hit a pothole. The glove-box sprung open. I reached to close it still driving hitting a second pothole. First thought was to slow down, followed by I must get the grader over to level the track, then my hand closed on something that crumpled.

I glanced across, a paper bag. Instantly knowing what it was and where it had come from. Without any other thought Bert flooded my mind.

It was stupid but I first thought what a pity he missed the pleasure he always got sucking on boiled sweets, leading to thinking how he straightaway sent a note to Nancy about Lucy's tea set, though he was upset and could hardly write.

I had to pull over as the tears just flowed.

Arriving at the house two hours late Dad took a strip off me for taking so long on a simple job. Away I went again. Mum had to comfort me and when she figured it between my sobs she sent a flummoxed Dad to do a job outside.

Over dinner he apologised, Mum empathized, while sis looked at me like I was joining Gran.

It was not all Bert did for us.

A letter arrived from Nancy.

In the same pink envelope the same perfume neat script.

Dear Walkaway family of my Bert,

Never wrote to him all his life and now I write twice in a few months. Can't be all that good you might think, first Lucy pops off then Bert does a runner, now what?

Well it's good news. Turns out I am Lucy's executor so I manage her will.

She left all her stuff to my Bert. Her solicitor's sorted it out, found she died pretty flush. Must have done alright out of property. Never told me much about her life before Bert but always seemed comfortable when Bert knew her. Her hubby was an accountant and liked houses for investment, kept being a secretary for a lawyer first then another accountant. Turns out she had the house she lived in plus three in Moonee Ponds. Rented them and had a tidy lump in the Bank. Supported a home for wayward girls too, just never can tell.

Bert's left all his stuff to your children. Solicitor says Lucy's money and houses goes straight to them. Couldn't think of a nicer family myself.

Send the solicitor the nippers details and he will fix it.

Seems a straight up and down old chap tho I don't know him, he's been doing Lucy's business stuff for ages. Took me out for afternoon tea, lovely toffee-nosed sort of place in the Windsor Hotel, never been there before, but very nice if I do say so one of them places Bert probably took her. Probably charged it to Lucy's account if I know lawyers, so only had one scone, but drained the pot.

Yours sincerely,

Nancy

or Dot as my Bert always called me

***

A paper clip attached the embossed business card of a solicitor in Flemington.

***

Sis got shitty showing she wasn't listening. She never really talked to Bert so thought she'd have got nothing special, maybe I should have given her a shake but didn't. I decided to talk to Harry about his money letting Mum sort Sis out. Mum said she'd get Dad to sort the money out.

My dreams began keeping me awake each night. I did everything from buying Warra, to horse stables, to motorbikes, flying to Europe to visit Yonke. Every night another one.

School was looming.

CHAPTER SEVEN

Do we really want more?

Before I grew up and got concerned, it had been the case that for years if anyone mentioned a nearby farm was up for sale, asking if we were interested, Dad would smile a wistful, sad sort of smile, usually replying 'Our debt's manageable, we've got a quid in the bank, son's not interested so why do we really need more dirt,' before he looked away in an embarrassed way. It took me a while to realise it was a sort of game he played with Mum, who never really became involved and like I say I was still a bit of a kid.

Months after Harry and Bert departed Dad was imbibing his favourite and only drug, other than the occasional single malt, his fortnightly bible the 'Stock and Station Journal. Like all addicts he would abandon jobs to collect it from the mailbox every Tuesday, as soon as it arrived, then settle into his favourite arm chair, with a cuppa and go off-air.

I could read it the day after, once he put it on the side table, before it was there no one touched it, not even Poppa. The Stock and Station Journal was the Bible in our house, you never questioned its facts. From cover to cover it was full of sale yard prices, properties for sale, information about breeding any animal you could name, and up to date technical stuff on all aspect of cropping.

For gossip it was invaluable too, with regular updates on who was doing what with whom. The Hatch Match and Dispatch Notices was Mum's territory who also read it for the recipes, after I was done.

There's a big section with details of farms for sale all over the State and recent property auctions which Dad reads with religious fervor.

The print would be pretty well read off it before Poppa got a go. He joked he only read the big print and comics anyway, so waiting wasn't a problem, 'Might take me all day to find where I put me reading glasses.'

After everyone had a turn mum gathered the loose sheets from all over the house. Some consigned to wrap veggie waste, some to assist the stove-fire lighting, then leftovers to the pile by the back door. The following Monday only the big print was still attached.

***

It was lunchtime before Dad looked up, cuppa in one hand, salad sandwich in the other, with his mouth full he asked the open room, 'Merle, the Jamieson's other block is up for sale, what d'you think?'

Cutting meat and veggies for a casserole Mum looked over her shoulder.

'I think you should empty your mouth before talking. Betty told me at church last week, must've forgotten to tell you, they'd like a bit over a thousand an acre.'

'Useful to know,' Dad ignored his admonition, 'it's for auction around that price it should be a good buy. Only a k from the block we bought off them they join down the back.' Scratching his stubble he read the advert again. 'Wonder why Graham never said anything? 'His cancer's got worse, needs radiotherapy down in the city. They've decided to take a break, stay down then head to the warm in the Gold Coast to stay with his sister. They're proud people, don't want word to get out how crook he is, and while we're on it you better have your check up too.'

'Strewth, I've known him since primary school you'd reckon he could tell me. I'll duck over today have a bit of a chat maybe we could share-farm it till he's better. Hate to see him have to sell it then regret it later, and yeh if you make me an appointment I'll pop in.'

'We could manage to straddle it,' Mum replied after a few seconds thinking, sounding like someone from an American sit-com when she added, 'It would be right neighborly to help them. Can I hop in with you? I'd like to have a good chat with Betty, we never get enough time after church. There might be more we can do to help, depends on how crook he is.'

***

Dad was happy to have company. He knows Mum's like me, quicker with numbers before they arrived she'd have worked out what it would earn after expenses and from that, what it was worth to us. Back when we were going to buy a computer it came up over dinner. Poppa commented 'Greg you've married a human calculator, why buy a computer when you've got Merle. I bet those things can't cook a roast like she can and do sums at the same time.'

Dad knew Jamieson's land was as good as ours, almost every hectare is arable, plus it grows excellent crops. For years there's been a competition to see who achieves the best yield. Walkaway uses stubble to grow-out our sheep. We used to burn it like the whole neighborhood but it was such a waste. Jamieson's don't carry many sheep and still burn-off, ash blowing away good soil nutrients, lots landing on our block. If the wind is weak, burns drop to a smolder with dense acrid smoke stinking for weeks.

After harvest vast golden fields of tall stubble reach to the horizon. Field mice breed like rabbits, kites and hawks float down from nests full of young, in trees on the stony ridges. In good years we bale tall stubble, selling to people who chaff it for the racing industry.

***

A while back no one was certain but now there's little doubt Gran's having trouble finding all her marbles. Since Harry left, then Bert died suddenly she seems worse, becoming so confused she can't even find her marble bag, let alone the marbles to put in it. At Bert's funeral she kept asking out loud who Nancy was, despite Mum telling her again and again. Nancy never got embarrassed, just smiled and moved to talk to someone else. Yet a few months ago she was as sharp as a tack and kept up with news, gossip and the state of the nation. Dad's found it hardest to cope with the changes.

Whenever we needed extra help Dad hired them on a short term basis, letting them camp in one of the many houses that litter our blocks, or drive home each night. Labour costs with Harry gone will increase but also help my chances when I'm home from school.

Bert packing up so suddenly threw issues into deeper confusion. As long as

I can recall we've gone without needing to hire full-time, suddenly with both Harry and Bert gone we might need two new staff to cope, considering the new blocks with the need for security, it's best staff live on site.

***

The early winter the series of unseasonably thick fogs and not planning for no Harry or Bert, we didn't get our best stubble taken off. It's going mouldy and becoming inedible, so this might be our year for a big burn after winter grazing, to keep the wheat viruses down, it will also let the drill and harrows have half a chance to cover the ground at seeding. Dad reckons barbequed mice might require a re-write of the hawk's usual menu.

***

The first reply to Dad's ad at Centrelink arrived by email, 'Have everything you want. Own transport. Live in Mingenew. Would like to meet as soon as possible. Paul z.' followed by a mobile number

'With a name like that he's probably one of them foreigners, probably a boat-people,' Dad suggested.

Mum messaged back inviting him out to meet and look at what we were offering.

As Walkaway's an hour from town so we thought he'd probably leave it and be out next day. A phone call five minutes after she emailed changed our view.

Forty five minutes later a bright red, late model Commodore burbled up. I thought two things, he must have driven pretty fast and Harry would love a car like that, even just to look at. Then I was staring my mouth open as an apparition unfolded from the front seat.

CHAPTER EIGHT

Tall as Paulz

Paul Z was tall as Dad, with a mess of straw-like hair, a sort of orange colour, as if a rinse had gone wrong, obviously used no conditioner and knew no decent barber. Big hands with long flat spatulate fingers, very noticeable as he waltzed up to Dad, right hand confidently outstretched in greeting. A waltz, not a stride, more a dance-step very light footed for such a tall man. I was close enough to hear his voice which sounded strange, a bit sing-song and not as gruff as his size suggested.

'Well nice to be here, how do I convince you to hire me. I like the look of the country and you seem like decent folk. So ask away.' Confident and chirpy.

They went inside leaving time to check out the car. Fully optioned 250hp motor dual pipes wide alloy rims coupled to low profile tyres. I was impressed by the badge; Berlina; the fit-out said flash. It was up to the folks.

Inside for an interminable time so I cleaned the Yammy spokes, wondering what questions they might be asking. I've no experience hiring staff so no idea how you go about it and couldn't think who Dad had ever hired. It was easy to see the result. Three quarters of an hour later our new employee came bouncing out. No waltz now, more a flounce attached to a vigorous stride. He shot across to his car did a u'ey and headed back to town, without a burnout which I was sure from the look on Dad's face impressed him more than whatever they'd discussed.

I had to wait until over dinner to be informed, because Mum headed into town behind the Berlina, Dad disappearing in his ute without comment. No point asking Gran, she was probably asleep, failed to have her hearing aid switched on or was still looking for her marble bag.

At dinner the interview and selection was number one topic courtesy of my questions. 'If I'm ever going to manage Walkaway I'll need to know how to hire and fire staff. What happened, how did you decide to choose him, and what are his terms of employment?' I thought it sounded as professional as a trainee manager should.

Dad seemed not to agree and kept his face directed at his plate, pushing a bit of curried cauliflower in circles.

Gran perked, 'Oh is there someone new coming?'

I told her, 'Yes Gran, we need a new station-hand to replace poor Bert and fill in for Harry.'

Not a glance from Dad, still finding his cauliflower curry most engaging. So it was going to be down to Mum as usual. Looking at me she started, This may be a test of just how grown up you really are. He did not get the job. She did.'

I sat speechless. I'd only seen one person arrive, go inside and leave, 'Did I miss something?' sounding as I felt quite bewildered.

'So is no-one replacing old Bert after all?' Gran piped in.

'Yes Mum we've chosen someone to replace Bert', sounding a little distressed it was going to be up to her, under pressure Dad failed to explain, 'His name is Paul and hers is Paulz.'

'Oh good, so are we getting two people? Dad always said Bert was worth two ordinary men.' Gran's mind was at least partly switched on: more than I felt.

'He's certainly no ordinary man,' that much is for sure Dad almost wailed.

'Gran can I explain it to you tomorrow, I think you sound a bit tired and we might need to talk about it,' Mum suggested, helping her toddle her off to bed after good-night kisses. She'd be a while, because Mum had to dress her for bed and do her teeth so I had an opening. 'All right Dad what's the G.O. It can't be that hard surely,' but his closed look said it was, he could not even look me in the eye, keeping his head down, hands on his knees.

I walked over and lifted his right hand up, holding it in mine, 'Is he a tranny? Is that it?' I pounced, sure I had stumbled onto the answer, but amazed that my father had actually engaged someone like that. Well not 'like that' but all the pieces fitted. Weird hair mincing slightly strange step then Mum's change of gender in mid-sentence, telling Gran she would explain later and Dad saying he was 'no ordinary man' nailed it.

It was the only answer.

***

'I don't know what you call him or her, but she told us she used to be a him and now him's a her or vice versa. Your Mum says what sex he is doesn't matter, it's what he or she can do that matters. Written references are impeccable, diesel mechanic's ticket, worked at John Deer's factory ten years, another ten at Co-operative Bulk Handling, plus a smattering of odd jobs. I'm glad that's over. Can't remember last time I interviewed someone for a job, not sure what our neighbors will say though.'

He let go of my hand to walk to the kitchen to put the kettle on, so I followed putting my arm around his fattening tum.

'So that's all it was. I guessed when he got out of the car, the way he waltzed over to you, the look of his hair, huge hands, voice. We did an assignment on transsexuals Dad. They're just people trapped in the wrong gender. God got his genetic traffic signals mixed up and they have to sort it out the hard way. It'll be OK if he has the skills and who cares what the neighbor's think. That's what you and Mum always tell me. Now let's see you practice what you preach.'

Mum appeared a minute later, slightly flustered and uncertain, with the kettle just beginning to whistle, her timing was impeccable.

'It's ok Mum I told Dad the answer so he didn't have to tell me. I'm glad you gave him or her a go. If the referees stack up, so what? It should be cool. I like the look of the car he drives and if I give her a few lessons in hair-sense I reckon it'll all be seriously cool. None of our neighbors are that switched on anyway, they probably won't even notice. Unless he goes into the wrong dunny at the footy,' and cracked up at my own joke, which no one found humorous.

***

You grow up thinking your parents are the font of all information until one day something like this happens, then you realise the world has passed them by. In the case of my Mum and Dad it happened while they were growing wheat to feed the ordinary's, gay's, lesbians and transexuals of the world. Well at least they'd taken a chance which blew me away.

Pity Harry's not here to do stuff with Paulz, they could share a heap in skills and with Harry to give him an intro Paulz would soon find a fit. Maybe when he comes back?

CHAPTER NINE

Yonke

I brought Dizzy as a pony, a quarter horse blood mare cross, we've won ribbons for barrel races and tent pegging, she needs work but gets less and less since I got the Yamaha. Mum figures I should find someone who will work her if I'm not going to. I know I don't put in enough time working her and can see she's getting fat, but don't want to sell her so should retire her.

***

My weekends hours are often spent out in the paddocks with my best girlfriend Yonke. We used to ride our horses, only occasionally using our one farm bike double dinkying as we checked sheep, cleaned troughs or repaired broken fences, a bit unsafe. Whether horses or bikes we did anything just to ride both Dizzy and Polo, Yonke's horse. Polo's camped on Walkaway to be always available, now she's also getting fat from not enough work. We talk lots about leaving the bikes in the shed and using the horses, but too often we take the easy route, though we do call them in to groom before dinner.

We try to swap sleep-over's, catching the Friday afternoon school bus out then getting a lift home on the Monday, in the return bus. We keep a full change of clothes at each house. At her place, we ride pillion on her Dad's old British four stroke 650cc BSA. A totally different bike it weighs a ton and takes a while to wind up but ma'ate it has such a beautiful four stroke exhaust note and a huge seat with soft springing. Her Dad never rides it so he's happy to let us.

Yonke looks slender where I look skinny. It must be an illusion because she's taller by a few centimeters and weighs a couple of kilos more, probably only because she's taller. We share shoe size, which makes for fun when we dress up. She has the look of a picture postcard Norwegian sailor, with far away crystal blue eyes and straight dark blonde hair down to her shoulder. My hair's almost brunette and now it's bobbed it's developed a curly mind of its own.

Her Mum's parents are Dutch and used to grow Tulips before they emigrated for a better life. Her Dad's family had always been doctors until he became a farmer, after he left Uni. She wants to farm too but has two elder brothers, so it's not clear how she'll get to keep her feet on their farm. We've talked about joining forces and farming together, at night imagine the furor two women living and farming together might create. I can hear local tongues wagging, then Paulz would really seem unimportant.

***

For a long time I've known but not understood how Dad sees my future with Walkaway, but it was clarified the other night. Yonke's Dad and Mum were talking with mine, after they'd driven over for dinner, staying to take Yonke home. I was in the lounge with her when I overheard Dad say, 'Now Harry's gone this might be the end of our line in the farming game.' I burst into the dining room, told him exactly what I thought, then ran out crying. The idea that all our history and hard work would be for nothing had me tossing all night with Yonke, who decided to stay holding me, telling me we'd sort it.

Her parents are more open minded than mine so she might have the chance that most times I don't think I have. Even with Harry gone and all I am doing Dad just can't see it.

***

As I came down the hall next morning grumpy and tired I checked the photos of the old family, hanging along the hall walls and over the lounge mantle-piece. They're reminders of the history of time, effort and hard work that have given us Walkaway, even if someone did lose the pastoral properties. I realise how strangely out of place the photos would look in a city house. They also remind me how much Harry looked like Grand-dad as a teenager. The rest of the tribe look different but Harry could have been Granddad's twin.

The wall of family photos in the lounge of Yonke's go some way to explain part of our family's entirely different perspectives on life. Hers show all sorts of different people from all sorts of professions. One shows a great uncle who was said to be mad, another two wild-haired scientists, others lawyers in wigs, with wives dressed in high society clothes of the times, some farmers are in high boots, in flat fields of tulips stretching as far as you can see.

Her photos are black and white or sepia, so you can't tell where her simply beautiful blue eyes entered the family tree. Annamie, her mother, says they were introduced by a Spanish ancestor, who also gave Yonke her fabulous permanent tan and remarkable aquiline nose.

***

Our other best friend is Manju. Our differences are striking. For a start Manju has a built in tan, that doesn't need a top up. A tea-pot shorter than Yonke and a chisel handle shorter than me, she gains height because she has the wildest, thickest, jet-black curly hair. It adds about 15 centimeters to her and shoots everywhere, unless she ties it with a ribbon. She came here as a refugee with her family from Sri Lanka, her family are Tamils but not Tamil Tigers.

Her Dad got a job in Geraldton as a G.P., retraining to make his Sri Lankan qualifications match Australia' requirements. I was glad to meet someone with a different view of the world, who was such fun and disproved all the stuff in the papers about Sri Lankans. Her Dad took a better job interstate in Gisborne, a Victorian town two hours from Melbournem, so Manju had to change schools. They shifted to Macedon so she's finished just around the corner from my Aunt and Uncle which just might affect my choice of secondary school as long as she stays put.

Her Mum has two skill sets, a dietician and a lab assistant at the Geraldton hospital. She was lucky to be offered a position with more exciting work as a research assistant in cancer research for children at the Peter Mac Cancer Hospital in Melbourne. So off Manju went and away went another best mate.

Because there was nowhere else to stable Isabella Manju left her here, so now

I'm the only one to ride her though it's a way to be certain I'll see Manju again. Izzy's a lazy old bay, mare after three foals she doesn't mind not getting lots of work, but she's getting fat as well. Manju intends to fly over whenever she can wangle it, which should at least be holidays and stay at whichever house for the two weeks. Then Izzy will get work, because there won't be enough bikes.

CHAPTER TEN

Just another block

Dad didn't reach an agreement to share-farm with the Jamiesons as they'd firmly decided to quit farming and focus on his health. He bought the two blocks of their farm at Auction, for a price less than he'd offered over a cuppa. It also meant we acquired their old houses and sheds and instantly had heaps more buildings, split between two different properties.

Dad drew the line at owning their tired old gear, no matter the price, so Jamieson's arranged a gigantic clearing sale before we took over. Buyers arrived from hundreds of kilometres away, driving trucks to immediately cart home whatever they purchased, because a condition of the auction was to clear the site two days after the sale.

Out of my pocket money I bought their Yamaha stock bike, for only a hundred and fifty dollars as no one else wanted it. I got it on my first bid, wondering if I'd put my bid in too quickly, and had I waited it might have come cheaper. Harry reckoned he could fix it up and did. Hee Haa!! I had a bike of my very own.

Buying Jamieson's meant we owned and Dad had to manage a truly huge property. Their furthest back corner was twenty kilometres from our homestead. Our back paddock gate became ten from our wool-shed. Some neighbour's fenced in lanes to help move sheep around, we didn't and Jamieson's didn't either, because they didn't carry many sheep. Dad never saw the value in the extra fences to maintain.

To properly amalgamate the two properties and make best use of the extra fencing, dams, bores, plus installing new yards was going to take a year or two and be complicated: but it got Dad excited again. I added forward planning to my skill set, strengthening my argument when I next tried again for trainee owner.

CHAPTER ELEVEN

Secrets

I don't have secrets from Mum, some from Dad, but usually just girl stuff. I didn't think Harry and I had any, but discovering his relationship with Alysha blew that lifelong theory out with the cobwebs. I felt I could tell Harry anything and know he'd keep it to himself and share, my little excitements with him gone, all I have is no one. My two best friends have left, Sis is hopeless, blabbing to Mum within minutes, she realises immediately and apologises, but as a consequence I never tell her anything.

Harry used headphones to Skype, as they were gone I figured he'd taken them, providing hope that he'd Skype once he got settled and got hooked up. I never told Sis. If Harry wanted to call her he could, but his cover would be blown on whatever he was doing. I thought he wanted space and time to find himself as well as to uncover the truth about the 'old business' denied us for so long.

I'd assigned him an old Claxton car horn as a special call signal, so I could pick it whatever time he called. The horn sounded late on a Friday night at the end of a long week with so much change at my end. With Sis in her room, headphones so loud, I could hear her latest acid rock CD and Mum and Dad down in the lounge. Maybe clicking the snib on my door was over the top but I wanted privacy. Hearing his voice gave me the shivers. It was magic and helped confirm any doubts about how much I missed him were unfounded.

'G'day fudge, finally got a connection. Need to try and get calls for free. I'd go broke with the number of times I want to tell you something and no Skype.'

The line dropped out, it's the real bummer with Skype which Harry says is just the price of FREE. Because our rule is the caller rings back I waited, so we don't both try at the same time and jam in the middle. Sure enough.

'Let's skip g'days everyone OK? We're both good. Bloody hot up her, day time up to mid 40's high 30's some nights. But we love it. This place is pure magic. Go online and check out the pics. It really is that beautiful. Mum and Dad would love it but chalets are a couple of grand a night so it's out of our world, unless you get a job like we did. Mainly the crew are all our age but NO partying is the rule.' The brief pause was my cue, 'Bert passed away quietly on his porch, got a letter from his sister just before saying Lucy had died. Nancy, his sister flew over for the funeral and stayed in his hut, wanting to see if Lucy missed something, decided not.'

He didn't come straight back so I grabbed the air-space.' We got a new station-hand to replace you and Bert you'll never guess what gender.'

'A chick, surely not the old man's not that progressive.'

'More even, a fair dinkum trans-sexual called Paulz. Worked at John Deere and has a serious dose of the smarts, shown Dad a few tricks with the Header already. Neighbours don't know but might get a shock if they give any cheek. Two metres plus hands like cleavers and a decent set of shoulders. Hottest V8 Berlina bright red, mags and dual pipes you'll love it.'

I could hear his gasp. 'You're taking the mickey what did Mum say? 'apparently stunned more by Paulz than the death of Bert.

'I think Mum pushed for him or her because of the references. She can do book-work too and likes gardening just needs a regular visit to a good hairdresser. Really nice person you'll get on well with when you get back.'

I should have picked the pause and worked out what was coming. 'Not sure I'll be back home for a while, we both love it up here and with keep chucked-in the money's good. Haven't met any trouble yet, but I doubt any of that mob could afford to hang around a place like this. Mainly tourists types. Boss reckons I'm magic cos of all the skills I have, says he hasn't had a worker like me before. Offered me the foreman's job and a better hut if I take a full year contract. Most staff are blowins and he wants someone to stay on for a while, suits us perfect. Don't tell the oldies, if we decide that way I'll ring and give the news myself. Maybe that will get them out of Ming to come up and see the place. You could tag along with sis. I could get you a special rate if it's not peak season.'

I heard the sound of the door being pushed and figured it would be Mum. 'Ducks on the pond call later love and miss you. Cheers to Alysha.'

Giving myself a few moments to collect my thoughts I headed to the door, walking out as if I was just going to make a cuppa, realizing I'd forgotten the inheritance. She must have had her ear to the door and almost fell in when I pulled it open, 'Sorry Mum, didn't know you were into eavesdropping.'

There was no point in fibbing, so she stood up and looked directly at me. 'Your door was locked, you never lock it, so yes I wondered what you were up to.'

Leaving her rhetorical question hanging unanswered I asked one of my own. 'You didn't answer my question.'

'I'm worried we haven't heard from Harry for weeks now anything could've happened.'

Mum you always tell us no news is good news, relax I'm sure he's ok if anything had happened he'd have rung, if something really bad happened the cops would've.

It took her a second.

'You would tell me if you heard from him wouldn't you, wouldn't you?' her voice loaded with anxiety. Ducking the question I hugged her and headed down the hall.

'If I had anything serious to tell you you'd be the first to hear.' Not as dumb as she can seem she saw straight through it, following me down the hall. 'And if something almost just about normal had happened?' I was there first, 'You'd be second,' walking to where the Yammy waited. I so needed to blow some cobwebs out, wishing Yonke was around. We both loved to ride at night with either one on pillion hugging the one in front.

***

It was nearly six weeks until I heard his voice again. Each day I waited I regretted not talking longer when I had him. El Questro was out of mobile range, so getting him on Skype depended entirely on his schedule, not mine. I figured it was punishment for something bad I'd done but couldn't figure what. Daily I desperately hoped the family saying that 'no news is good news' was correct.

CHAPTER TWELVE

Shearing

Even as a kid I've been excited by busy times. Chances to do stuff, even just sweeping the wool floor during shearer's tea breaks. Being responsible has always given me a buzz. It's always been annoying when good things happen during school time, on School of the Air I was always grounded until school-work was completed so the best set-up was to arrange with Poppa to make sure all jobs were after the school bus drop. Folks are ok as long as homework gets done so TV's a no-no. Neither Mum nor Dad let me stay home from school or do jobs unless I run a temp then if I actually get crook they actually make me stay in bed so it's never been worth pretending.

I'm not dumb, I realised early the jobs I got weren't critical, but I found happiness being trusted to handle them if something went wrong and now tick them off the skills list needed to be a manager.

When working with Poppa he just gives hints about how or why, then lets me work it out but never takes over, instead he lets me be boss, even letting me boss him. He explains in ways that help me understand why you do something a particular way, so later I can work out what's the best choice for me. Dad did it that way with Harry when he was home, though with me there are still times when he acts as if I should already know or that it doesn't matter whether I know why, as long as I can do the job.

Without Poppa I've learnt not to bother Dad for the few things I don't know, I just take extra time to figure out how. If I got stuck before I used to just go to

Poppa who made time to chat as well with him taking permanent long service leave I'm forced to make my own decisions. Maybe now you can see why I lost the plot on the verandah.

***

Shearing happens once a year, crutching in between, with a bit of luck both happen during school holidays. The best job at both is mustering mobs, into the woolshed then back to their paddocks when they're done, jobs Bop and I can do alone. Our sheep are put to graze in separate paddocks once they've been sorted into age or gender based mobs. When mustering or moving between paddocks it's important to not let them get mixed and also to bring them into the yards in the right order for shearing.

The year I turned eleven Poppa and I had planned to get up early, so Mum made us a big breakfast, packing smoko and lunch, putting a thermos of hot water in for tea. I was competent on the bike so we took both the Ute and a motor bike out to muster our biggest paddock. Poppa had long since given up riding the bike, commenting his bones were too old for the jarring it gave his rattly joints. Anyway that day he was happy in the Ute listening to farming news. I used to kid that he listened to the Country Women's Hour to write down the recipes. That usually got a chuckle before a cuff round the ears when he told me not to be cheeky to my elders. A joke neither of us tired of.

We drove out in convoy, I didn't ride behind, there was usually too much dust so instead I rode off to one side and arrived first, responsible to open and shut gates. They can't be left open in case sheep wander through and mobs become mixed. Shutting gates behind you is a golden rule, if I do the gates Poppa can stay in the ute and not strain himself.

We needed to bring our largest mob in from the Big Paddock way out back. The family never got all that excited about giving names to our paddocks so they've all got boring names like Green-gate, Hard-water, Red-tank and so on.

Harry couldn't help, he was flat out drenching with Dad, and once done he'd have to walk that mob back out, before mustering another paddock to bring yet another mob in. As it was a scorching mid-summer day and our mob was made up of our oldest ewes with young lambs at foot we'd have to travel them very slowly. You should never make sheep do more than plod unless you want to risk them overheating, so travelling a mob of ewes and lambs in from out back can take a whole hot day. It's critical to ensure lambs don't lose touch with their mothers when walking in so far.

Lambs are like little kids and love playing 'I am king of the castle', leaping off rocks and logs and playing chasey while poor old mum plods on ahead ignoring them searching for a green pick as she goes.

Poppa reminded me that lambs only have their mum for a fluid supply so unless you give the mob a break lambs won't get a drink once the mob's travelling. A lamb hat doesn't drink for a few hours can die from heat exhaustion.

To make sure a mob only walks as fast as they want to you must keep well back making sure the dogs also hang back. Sometimes you let the mob dawdle and don't chivvy them up. It's times like that when your dog training shows. Then dogs need to just sit or stay, not keep roaming back and forward behind them mob as that will just stir them up.

Dogs can have their excitement once the sheep are yarded and need to be forced into the shed or through the drafting gates Poppa would advise over and over.

***

Every time a mob is shifted out of a paddock you need to count them to make sure you've found them all in your muster and none are left behind. Poppa was brilliant at counting sheep running through a paddock gate so good city visitors often didn't believe it. He could count four at a time as they leapt and raced though each sheep dumbly hoping there was something better on the other side.

When counting it looked as if he was directing an orchestra waving his hand in the air like a conductor while mentally slicing them into small groups as they surged through. Watching as we left the paddock that day I commented. One day I'll be as clever as you are and Bop will be the equal of Buster. Giving his lazy smirk he countered.,

It takes a while. You first have to get good at counting in fours really fast but you're improving. High praise for a kid and enough to keep me trying. I practiced at every opportunity counting singly or in twos while they ran out of the off-shears pens, where they could only run through a small gate, counting the same sheep again two at a time when they were let out the back gate of the yards on their way to a fresh paddock. Counting them at all off shears was a waste of time as we knew the numbers from the tally off the board but it was practice and I knew immediately if I got a count wrong. Dad had noticed already and commented before Poppa did.

You're improving porridge. High praise from the real boss was worth a lot more.

***

One thing after another had delayed us that day late leaving so even later getting the mob to the first gate on their way back. Poppa counted while Bop and I pushed them up. When the last sheep had run through, Poppa looked worried, hustling forward to shut the gate shut. I asked. 'Why the frown?'

'Count's one short, an ewe must have died since last shift.'

'You know older ewes die during lambing but I felt certain I'd have seen a fresh carcass,' so offered, 'I could rip around and check again there's a bit of scrub so I might've missed one,' Poppa considered for a second, 'I'm sure between them the dogs would've seen every sheep and fetched them all, but have a quick loo, lucky you've got the bike not Dizzy' as an afterthought he advised, 'Remember to tell Dad to change the paddock-book if we don't find it, he needs to record a sheep has died.' You can claim dead sheep for taxation.

Heading to do a quick sweep with Bop propped high on the tank I travelled counter clockwise, heading to patches of bush an eye out for circling crows or eagles. They're early indicators of a sheep in distress sure enough an eagle gave me the bearing. Right back where I'd started the muster.

Fifty metres inside the gate stood a patch of thick scrub. I remembered thinking the main mob would be miles away near the big dam. I wouldn't make that mistake again. My blunder my problem to fix it and remember not to do it again.

'Found her Poppa, back near where I came in. On her side, with twins. I'd prop and leave her, but there's an eagle hanging around. Call you back,' I rang in on the mobile.

I tried propping her on bits of scrub then rocks and finally pushed up a piece of rotten log. She kept falling as she continued to struggle to get on her feet, the lambs bleating their distress. I knew if I left them either the lambs or the ewe would be attacked by the eagle or marauding crows and we'd lose all three.

Bop gave me the idea. She began to push the lambs in close, forcing by just using eye, a real thrill as it's something a working dog either does or does not, you can't teach them. It's one of those things that I used to joke about the dogs brain getting full of, and here was Bop showing she had it.

Once the pair were close and nuzzling the old girl's udder she sat and watched as the old girl lay quietly on her side, content now her lambs were quiet and the pressure was off her bulging udder. It's what old Renee would have done, so maybe the genealogy thing was true the habit just needed an opportunity to come good.

Still on the bike I patted Bop and told her to stay, her least well-developed skill but I had no other choice. If she followed I could try and send her back, if she stayed I could be back in an hour to collect the lot of them. It seemed worth the chance.

***

Circling back I joined Poppa and told him my plot. He pushed on quietly, about lunchtime he suggested a cuppa we had a ways to go but he offered. We'll have a short camp, let the mob drift along the fence line, then catch them in time to push them through the next gate.

It was so hot I knew Bop would need a drink as much as we did. We always made sure we had extra water when we're out mustering, because you can never tell what might happen or how long a job will take and you always consider how hot a dog will get, they can't tell you.

Poppa got a morning-smoko out while I watered Bop, splashing my own face to cool down a bit. I was hungry and the sandwiches Mum'd made looked pretty inviting but I knew Bop would be getting anxious. I squatted next to Poppa, cheekily asking whether he could walk the mob while I took a drive in the ute.

My actual suggestion was. We're only having smoko because there's nothing good on Country Hour. Smartly put back in my place with, 'You got any more intelligent questions to ask?' He was hot and bothered too, so I zipped my lip and squirmed out by rejoining, 'I was worried your gammy leg might not be up to walking the mob until I returned you don't use the bike and it's pretty hot even sitting here.'

He nodded, so I packed up driving off while he was finishing his cuppa, wanting to get out and back before the mob made it to the next gate. With Buster working slowly and if his gammy leg held up, I hoped he wouldn't find it difficult to keep the mob together until the gate. Looking back I saw he had already lifted the mob and had them heading to the shed before dark.

Taking every short-cut I hoped Bop wasn't up to mischief or in trouble, I knew I was testing her limits and with only Buster's help Poppa could have his work cut out moving the mob if they got cranky.

***

Even after so long away when I burst through the scrub and saw her Bop was still sitting patiently, I grinned. I knew Poppa was probably already nearly pooped so I didn't muck around feeling proud. Using my knee to assist I hoiked the three of them into the tray-back of the ute one by one the fat ewe first. It took me two goes, the first to get her off the ground onto the log, the second up on my knee before onto the tray.

Noticing Bop was looking tired, with her tongue lolling she was letting me know she was thirsty again, I ripped my hat off, filling it from the tank. I watched as she guzzled a hat-full and asked for more. She didn't drink the whole of the second one so I threw it at her in fun and took off.

It's taken a long time to realise, but I know the way you see the world changes without you noticing. Bop had always known what to do, she just needed a chance and I'd never given her one, it occurred to me I could try again to convince Dad; maybe he just needed another chance.

***

Mum had our meals ready by the time we'd walked the sheep into the woolshed back yard, putting the ewe and lambs in a hay-bale yard inside the shed, heading inside for a wash up. Along with Dad Mum listened intently as Poppa bragged about how clever Bop was because of her breeding. I sat silent knowing it was my training.

I was pretty tired so I took off early to bed. Mum came in before I was asleep with a cuddle and a warm Milo. 'Bop was smart, Dad and I are proud of you for making the decision to not leave the old girl alone.' Dad even came in as he went off to bed, gave me a quick cuddle and at a glance silently said how proud he was. 'Good choice Pudding dog's improvement paying back your training made a good choice today.' Disappearing down the hall with his noisy boots.

Talk about earning bragging rights I thought as I drifted off. Wait until Harry heard. Alone again I must have lay thinking of the worst things that could have happened, before dozing off still worrying. I woke in the warm dark without switching my brain into gear. I ran out in my pajamas and slippers to see if Bop had run back to her kennel, I'd dreamt she was still out with the ewe and lambs.

She sat up looking sleepy, food bowl still full, but water bowl empty, I filled it and hugged her before heading back to bed. The air was nippy though but no wind to make it cold. The family snuggled in loose hay inside the woolshed would see the night out in more comfort than out in the paddock.

CHAPTER THIRTEEN

Paulz gets a wig

Dad's pride and joy is our Case harvester, a giant red machine with a dozen levers and myriad buttons, plus of course an air-conditioned cabin. Each harvest Poppa reminds us that in his day you just sat on your tractor in the dust, no fancy sealed cabins with air-conditioners. Dad laughs and bounces back, 'In that case it's a pity someone invented air-conditioned cabins because we'd probably be able to grow an extra crop in your lungs; they'd be so full of dirt and grain dust by now.'

You climb a vertical set of steps, swing the cabin door open then sit in the cabin. About five meters above ground, you can see forever. It's easy to get a bit distracted watching galahs and cockies flying in, collecting the fallen grains. I particularly love watching the elegance of various hawks just below the clouds, gliding in vast arcs peering down for mice in the stubble.

There are moments of deadly excitement as a hawk folds their wings, plummeting in a silent vertical dive, pulling out at the last split second, moments before it crashes. The last few metres are swept centimeters off the ground from where it takes a couple of lazy flaps before it flies to the nearest dead tree or sweeps upward to a nest high on the ridge, a motionless mouse clutched in vicious claws.

It's cruel but its nature field mice are certainly not endangered, it's also quicker than the mouse poison we spread around the silos.

***

Before my investment in fun, buying my own Yammy, I rode Dizzy for every job away from the homestead, fun but at a less dramatic pace. Poppa took the ute so we could carry things from job to job. I've got my own saddle, a Barcoo Poley, the saddle I used to ride stock-work for both barrel racing and tent pegging. While I can't do it, it's possible to rope from one, tho' mine doesn't have a roping horn, so it's not the correct saddle for real cattle work.

Dad owns an American roping saddle and can throw a lariat when he remembers how. A very different saddle from the Barcoo, with long flappy stirrup straps and squared off wooden stirrups, I'm allowed to borrow it as long as I clean it after each ride, another of his pride and joys seldom used.

He's happy the more stock work I do the more he doesn't have to. There's always heaps of his sort of work just keeping the place going. Mechanical stuff like fitting new blades on the harvester, adjusting the hay-baling machine, plus endless oiling and greasing, ensuring everything's in good condition and doesn't break down when the pressure is on and it's needed.

YUK not for me.

Dad and Bert ensured all maintenance was completed in the off season, so things didn't break down at critical moments when seeding or cropping was going full-bore. Maintenance jobs are boring so I duck out of the way when someone looks at me.

I'm uncertain who will help but I expect Paulz alleged skills will be put to the test.

***

I got to take him on a guided tour days after he started, making sure to tell him the night before to bring a food pack and the makings of his own tea or whatever. I turned up to his cottage not surprised to see him hoik a gorgeous wicker picnic basket into the tray, what did mildly surprise me was his request.

'Can I drive and you direct. That way I'll get a quicker grip on how the place is laid out.' I straight away remembered that was exactly how I felt when learning, Poppa always agreed so why not.

A careful driver, he was also an acute observer, unlike our casuals, who never spotted anything until it hit them, then couldn't care unless the sky fell in.

'So explain why that paddock looks as if it's been left fallow while the one next door is tall stubble,' was his first question.

They continued all day. Well thought out, not engaging mouth before putting brain into gear stuff. It was apparent quickly she had a smattering of farming knowledge but not much at depth. That matched what she'd claimed.

By smoko we were chatting easily, questions becoming more personal and acute as we drove across the block. 'Why did Jamiesons sell up their place looks comparable to Walkaway?' a good example.

Dying of cancer didn't elicit some stupid response. That's bloody tough on a chap, no kids to pick it up?'

His voice changed tone and modulation constantly, something I wasn't used to at home. We pulled in at the stockyards out near Fisher's well where Dad and Poppa had built a timber-framed shade over a slab of concrete, to make it easier to work during hot weather. Fisher's Well because the water borer was, you guessed it, Mr Fisher.

There's a wooden bench table and seat and stone fireplace to set a billy on, we had my thermos so decided not to set a fire given the hot dry weather. 'So are you going to stay on?' his first bald question to me.

'Are you?' I countered, unsure of wanting to give much away just yet.

'Look, I don't play word games. Once I came out I made sure I was always up front. Some folk don't like it, that's their right but I never lead them up the path.'

I'd never met anyone so upfront before and didn't quite know how to proceed.

'You can ask me anything and I'll answer you truthfully. You may not like some answers but you'll soon find out who I am. Your folks did and here I am. What would you like to know ask away,' in that singsong voice neither fully male or fully female. A big breath and, 'I know a bit from school about tranny's but can you explain it your way.' She looked at me hard probably to make sure I was not being frivolous. 'Well let's start as we intend to finish. Tranny is not how I describe myself. I describe myself as transsexual in the same way you call yourself a girl or a female. I was labeled a boy as a child because I had a penis. I never felt comfortable with that label and tried to hide the reason. As an adult I went to a clinic to find I had an x/y chromosome disorder. My body expressed it as male in terms of my genitals but my brain didn't like it. For the last ten now I've lived entirely as a female, despite an almost masculine body. Before you ask I don't intend to have it chopped off, a large percentage of blokes who do go on to commit suicide, I enjoy my life too much for that, I take hormone tablets.'

Her voice remained strong and clear with no call for sympathy. Gob-smacked and impressed I wasn't sure I'd have had that much courage with a stranger. 'So why Paulz why not Pauline or something?'

'My mother was Pauline Dad was Paul. They're both dead but I figure this way I show my pride and the acceptance I found from both of them. I came out just before they died, they both accepted me without any question. Wish I'd done it earlier. It was so much easier than I had hoped.'

'Must've been hard. Did you live at home before?'

'Before, since, all my life, I never saw a reason to shift, except to do my apprenticeship, still own the same house, chose to rent it and travel.

'You certainly put it out there, so can I make a couple of comments.'

'Of course you can.'

'I reckon you should get a better wig. one that matches your skin colour. The one you have is all wrong for your skin colour, and pardon me, but while I am at it your breath smells pretty bad,' I'd wondered if I'd gone too far

In a totally different voice, something like the drag queen in Priscilla Queen of the Desert, Paulz answered equally bluntly. 'Well pardon me for living dahling,' with a limp-wristed display of her right hand.

'Sorry if I was rude, but I'd be happy to go to town with you and choose a new wig. I sort of specialize in looking at people's faces and bodies and working out stuff about them. My girlfriends all come to me for fashion advice, hair colours and stuff like makeup. It's just a gift I suppose.'

I didn't realize how presumptuous I must have sounded until that night when I was talking to Mum about the day and she pulled me up.

'You're on now. one's ever offered before and it's time I got a new one. When do we go?' then seemed to think for a bit. N'ot sure what to do about the teeth thing I never notice, is it that bad? 'Well it's not nice and might put people off you if they get close enough.'

***

The drive in was easy, she told me about her life as a kid, her family and her employment. Left school at fifteen before doing TAFE, because she was sick of being teased and still had not discovered the reason. Since then she'd worked as a female, but in male-dominated careers, testing both her capabilities and her ability to withstand bullying. Seeing Dad's advert on a Centrelink notice-board she came on a whim.

***

Though it was getting toward lunch there was one job we hadn't got around to. I had kept an eye on the weather, so we turned onto the old stock route running between us and our new Jamieson's block. A poorly maintained dirt track few neighbours use, so I didn't expect anyone but booming over a rise came a white Subaru ute, just about airborne as it leapt over the crest.

I knew who we were about to meet, the neighborhood hoon, from a family of no-hopers a slackarse lay-about and major gossip. I had thirty seconds to warn Paulz.

'Keep inside, don't talk he's a chatterbox and yobbo.'

She did as I asked, while Jeremy Davis skidded across in front of us, so he pulled up on my side anyway, no real risk.

'You're low flying today. I'm surprised to see you on this track. It's well out of your way. Something I should know about.'

Looking at us his shifty eyes darted around struggling to not stare as he tried to decide whether to get out or drive on. I helped him decide.

'Can't stop Jeremy got an appointment, knock you two down next time,' casually waving as an intro, watching him take off in a shower of gravel mist of dust.

'He'll find out soon enough, a stupid busy-body, never works, always has a dollar to party with. Everyone says his father subs him, but no one knows where his Dad gets it from either. I don't spend any more time with him than I need to,'

'Hey, your social life is your own. I don't expect you to plug me into everyone we meet. He doesn't exactly look like my sort', and chuckled, whatever sort that is.

The rest of the drive we discussed what she needed in the new wig, and I told her who the family dentist was. 'It might just be something that needs a scrape or it might be serious, you don't want an extraction if you can avoid one.'

I'd decided to write the rest of the day off and poke on into town. The hairdresser who stocked wigs was the same place I had my long hair cut and sold, she still kept my hair tidy. Allison welcomed me and scarcely turned a hair when I introduced

Paulz with, 'My new friend is a transsexual and wants a new wig. Do you have something nice that matches her skin colour.'

An hour later we walked down to the Coffee Palace, where I ordered an iced coffee and Paulz a long black, double shot. I tasted hers and nearly died, revolting! She made the same comment about what she called my sweet confection. It made us both crack up which is how my worst enemy found us when she swanned in.

Paulz now looking totally glam in her new bobbed cut wig, in dark brown natural hair a thousand dollars poorer which hadn't seem to faze her, almost looked cute for a big girl, a bloke could fall for her.

'Who's your new friend,' Jamie Douglas asked in her sickly sweet tone, sitting uninvited openly seeking answers.

'Let me introduce Paulz, our new station hand. Be nice or I'll let her eat you publicly,' I warned.

'Oh you wouldn't,' she squeaked looking at Paulz, 'Oh daahhling, I so would, I love embarrassing bitches.'

That stopped Jamie dead, she stood up and walked out, without looking back, glowing in embarrassment, while we cracked up in giggles and went on chatting, not wasting a second discussing her.

***

On the way in I'd rung Mum, who'd managed to get Dr R Fang, as I called him, to squeeze in a late afternoon appointment for Paulz. We had time to burn so loitered around the shopping strip, Dr Fang's real name was Dr Len Edwards but that seemed too normal for someone who spent his life looking for rotten teeth, so I'd long ago given him a new name. The R is for rotten.

Turned out it was nothing major, Paulz was just given a tooth clean with a microwave machine, and a lesson in good dental hygiene. Walking out she breathed on me and it smelt a heap better. Jobs done, friendship strengthened.

While I waited I'd started to wonder why Jeremy was flogging along the stock route. No easy answers came to mind, so I let it go and bought myself a bag of jelly snakes, not caring about Dentist's bills.

***

A few hours of summer daylight left we headed home, to tarp over the last heap of paddock-stored wheat. It was out near where I'd let Paulz drive a few days earlier. Because of no Harry and no Bert, one middling sized field-heap of wheat had still not been covered. Dad didn't think it was as much of a crisis as getting some stubble cut and baled to fill a cash contract. I disagreed and just then the distant blackening sky looked to be on my side of any discussion.

Without consulting Dad I decided Paulz and I would have to do it. It couldn't make things worse and I just might earn a gold star. It should have been a six-person job but I had Paulz with her big shoulders and me with my rat cunning. The poly tarp to cover a heap of wheat is vast, looks much huger and always feels twice as heavy. I wouldn't have tried, except the heap had already been partly covered, the balance of the tarp left lying in a flat roll across the top; but still frightening to think about dragging with just the two of us.

Paulz was about to show her Case talent and farming courage.

CHAPTER FOURTEEN

My lesson

Some sounds on a farm curdle your blood others warm you through strangely it can be the same sound but on different days. How you react depends on the time of year. On a tin roof rain starts with almost noiseless plops, becoming faster or slower, lighter or heavier depending on the clouds. If it gets heavier and heavier until it's teeming down, it becomes a deafening roar. Then you know either you have a good season break, or if the crops aren't off you've lost a fortune. Rain's the making or breaking of every season and every farmer, which is why they talk about it forever and seasons are remembered, by the rain that did or didn't fall.

***

This day almost all the grain was under cover, our stubble pretty well buggered, despite Dad's efforts. Except for the huge Case header, which I remembered Dad abandoning in the paddock, to do some stupid little job I thought all machinery was under shedding. So half a million dollars sat rusting in the paddock until he remembered. We were already at the break of the next season.

Not how I will run the place. It was a reasonable date for an early break of season but in true 'old business' fashion Dad misjudged it.

***

Heading out of town the odd huge single drop splattering our windscreen, I moaned. Dad flat out getting almost mouldy stubble cut and baled to fill a possible contract. We can't help him but he doesn't think the rain is close. I do and

Google weather supports me, as do those drops. Somehow we need to try and cover the rest of that heap quickly.

Flogging out of town Paulz commented dryly. 'Havn't had a bucket load of experience tarping heaps, can't be that difficult for two shielas,' and gave that throaty chuckle. I matched her style 'Be easier if I'd let you drag Jamie outside and asked her to help.' Getting in on the game he chuckled, 'There must be a way to get the grain under cover with just two of us,' smiling across the cabin a sweet breathed smile.

She changed view when we arrived. 'Hell the tarp must weigh a ton, you feel like some weightlifting practice.'

At moments like this I know why I should go to the shed each night and pick up Dad's old weights. 'We only have to drag the last quarter over, the tarp's concertina-rolled on top waiting for us.'

Paulz walked, checking how the tarp was fixed, estimating weights and heights above ground-level. Grain tarps are huge, blue reinforced plastic. Heavy, cumbersome and waterproof. Fortunately Dad buys concertina-folded tarps which, once you drag them out lay like huge blue folded sausage skins, you just have to flap over as the heap expands. Sounds simple with a team to help

Three-quarters had been covered as harvesting proceeded and as usual my forward-planning, failing to act, Dad had already dropped the white concrete anchor blocks. They are put on the low side, with walls to stop the grain sliding out endlessly. Just hadn't finished the job, deciding to do something else first. The 'old family failing' I thought, trying to see how to manage the job while ignoring constant slow lumps of wet-sky, making themselves felt by falling on me.

'We need to flop the balance of the blue sausage down to the far end, without tearing the tarp or dragging the grain with us. You can't climb a heap because it all comes sliding down underneath you. Normally you'd have all hands on deck to drag each new flap over, walking on the heap and shouting a lot.'

With a grin he laughed, 'where I come from two are seldom called a mob.'

Two was a fraction of how many we needed, but Dad was k's away, Harry in the Kimberley, Bert in Heaven Mum in town Gran hunting for her marbles. The blue-black approaching storm front loomed closer by the minute. Much longer the tarp would be too wet to walk on or handle. I could feel I was getting frightened and couldn't see any answer. I knew I'd stopped thinking clearly and had to get a hold on myself, so followed Poppa's advice when I got agitated, 'Swallow a cup of cement, mix with a cup of tea and harden up.' Paulz smiled at the advice, his face said he had nothing to lose and was not in a panic, he was thinking clearly.

'Is the Case header parked in the next paddock.'

I knew Dad hadn't shifted it, it would still be out there until he remembered it needed pre harvest maintenance and was driven in, but not until after the battery had to be disconnected, recharged then taken back, after the diesel lines were blown out and the whole machine de-spider webbed.

'Can you drive it,' looking at me hopefully.

There was little point in pretending at a moment like this, 'Had a few goes, but not really. ' Should be able to drive up to the heap, camber the comb to gate-clearing height, with one of us on it, jump off to scrabble as far as possible, then reach and roll the tarp over. Once that's under way the driver gently tilts the comb the other way when the silly bugger up top rolls the tarp onto the other side. Sound possible.'

Her smile is more like a smirk.

It did sort of, I had no other better idea and was aware of more than the occasional spatter of increasingly heavy drops so agreed hesitantly. 'Let's give it a crack.'

Actually I suggested Paulz gave it a crack, he was the Case expert. The engine fired immediately, with a slight wheeze the hydraulic pumps filled and the wide comb lifted to travel position. With only a hundred and fifty meter drive he spun it in its own length, enough to see he knew what he was doing.

I'd already dragged open the chain-wide wire gate, expertly he drove confidently toward the uncovered edge of the heap, me running behind. He braked, lowered the comb to let me climb up, yelling over the motor, 'OK what now, 'It has a canted position for clearing gates that's much higher than for travelling, hang on while I give it a go.'

I stood over the engine.

Up up and away I went, the comb slowly leaning at a huge angle until I was hanging on for grim death, nearly level with the top edge of the heap. I waved him to come-in and hung on as the harvester crept slowly forward. Once over the edge, part way up the tarp I climbed off, immediately sinking up to my knees in slippery grain. Grabbing a tarp-edge I began tummy crawling to the far end of the rolled tarp. Hand after hand I crawled, flopping it open. I went as far as I could before scrambling back to the comb's front edge which Paulz had driven up. Once happy I waved to back-up, feeling the comb tilt the other way as he selected reverse and headed to the other end to repeat his trick. Each flop the blue sheet slipped further over the grain, without a major mess, though with lumpy creases in the middle.

Once clear I was lowered.

We both clambered up the last metres to drag the middle out square and tight where the rolls were rucked in the middle. We slid off like two kids at a game park to examine our work, not perfect but mostly the heap was covered. Like the same two kids we cheered ourselves, high fived a job well done then got serious dragging the tarp edge ropes out to reach the concrete anchor blocks left out weight the edges down.

We tied it off as raindrops hit us with increasing anger but no sense of panic.

For a permanent fix Dad would need to dig a trench around the edge and tuck the tarp under, backfilling for a vermin-proof sealand to prevent the wind lifting it. I'd covered the heap, knew I had shown courage and wisdom and hoped I might score a gold star. Emptying grain out of our boots we headed home, maybe ten minutes daylight to spare, the road becoming muddier each minute.

So exhausted I could hardly lift my arms I felt good knowing I'd broken a family jinx, taken a chance and got the job done, unlike Dad farting about with mouldy stubble that at best would fetch a few hundred dollars, while the heap saved would be worth thousands.

***

Show you a shortcut to beat the storm I yelled, heading him across the next paddock. Driving toward the back gate I noticed a circular galvanised iron field bin leaning slightly. Tapping him I pointed to drive over and stop. I spotted the problem quickly. The bin had been dragged with a flat tyre and bogged, bending the steel rim in the process, not something even Dad would do.

I checked the tracks of the bin, a full bin would need our dozer to drag it and I was still unclear why anyone would have tried. Unsure whether we'd filled both bins in nthe paddock or just taken them out to the paddock in case they were required. I knew field bins are not designed to pull across ploughed ground, they're just temporary storage until the rail sidings bins are available.

Even Paulz could see them.

Glaringly obvious towing tracks made by a dual axle truck with tandem wheels. Dragging the bin with a flat tyre, in soft ploughed dirt meant it ploughed its own furrows before bogging, and whoever did it drove off.

My curiosity well up Paulz didn't understand until I explained how thing were done normally.

He understood quickly.

Dark approaching fast and twenty k's out Mum's dinner imagined pretty good to our hungry guts. My body was beginning to ache from the scrabbling and dragging but Paulz wasn't complaining.

First things first, we had to work out what had happened.

***

The stock route alongside the paddock showed where someone cut the fence, bent a couple of star pickets, drove in, tried to tow the bin, bogged it then drove out.

First question who now answered, second was why? Paulz cleared some scrubby stuff where the fence was pulled down, to make sure the ute could clear it, took ten.

Ten minutes to figure out who and why.

We could see the tracks heading away down the stock-route. I didn't understand why or where, the only place down the track was a deserted shack, unoccupied forever.

We headed after the tracks in fading light, Paulz fairly flying but with no fallen branches and the track well formed we hummed into the impending wet gloom. Ten k's down our answer was parked. A dark-green dual axle MAN twenty years old and scruffy, in its day a fair enough truck, still hooked on was another of our field bins Walkaway branded around it, an idea of Dad's in case someone stole them.

Good idea Dad, someone's just done it.

No-one was in it but the papers in the glove-box gave a clue as to who might have driven it. A license renewal in the name of Jeremy Davis, our neighbor in the Subaru, never had a job but always a dollar.

The key was still in the ignition but the wicked side of my mind had a better idea than driving it.

'Any hot water left in your fancy tea set?' I asked, on my knees and searching each ute tyre for a valve remover.

'If you ask nicely I MIGHT lend you some,' Paulz replied, taking the mickey after my comment about his 'fancy' tea set. Every sensible truck driver fits one valve remover as a valve-cap. On one of the eight wheels there had to be one, because the ute had none. I'd remedy that tomorrow.

Valve remover caps are used to change a valve because with one you can remove a valve speedily, anywhere without one it's a trip to the shed to find one.

' Spin the ute around and shine the headlights' I asked Paulz. There was one covered in dust, exactly what I needed.

'Start removing all valves , every one in your pocket we're taking them with all us, Sorry about the rain', beginning to pelt down.

Paulz, doing as I asked, went to the truck's side-saddle petrol tank, removed the cap, pouring in his gifted thermos hot water. It would do. Water and petrol don't work well when they arrive at the spark plugs. Because it's heavier and the two don't mix, water settles on the bottom, getting sucked up first. Engines don't run well on water, that MAN was going no-where fast but if whoever owned it came back they'd know someone was onto them. Assuming they fixed the tires, ten k's down the road the engine would cough splutter and stop, the fuel filter full of H_2O.

That MAN would not go far even if Jeremy drove on flat-tyred rims to escape.

A pocket full of valves and empty thermos we headed home laughing like kids. Between choking laughter Paulz wheezed, 'The best fun since I was a kid on Guy Fawkes night lighting penny-bungers, dropping them in neighbour's letter boxes and running.

The image started another fit of laughter.

Full of excitement that this time I'd done it, we headed for dinner.

***

'You're a right pair of hoodlums, hoons and vandals', Dad went off as a drier Paulz sat with us for a scratch dinner and we recounted our day. Too late to send him to his cottage to start his own tea he'd blow dried his new wig and got into some of Dad's gear, which fitted well enough.

The pile of valves in pride of place in the centre of the dinner table as Dad went on.

'Well done I need to ring Sgt Hanbury to get him onto the job as quick as. We might need to show him where it is as soon as we finish dinner and laughed. I'd never given them much to laugh about but both parents were instantly laughing, although worried about what Mum called my sudden criminal tendencies, as if I'd never been naughty. Compared to Jeremy I was innocent abroad.

Not a whisper of real praise, not a moment of accepting my commitment to the farm or my ability to think outside the box.

Without warning I saw red.

'I'm sick and tired of your attitude to me Dad. It doesn't even occur to you it was you left that heap out to weather for months while its value plummeted. You never drove the Case in under shelter and then despite our computer having the weather Ap you kept no eye on our weather. Today, despite more profitable options, you spent all day mowing and cutting second or third grade chaff from a paddock of mouldy stubble, for which you'll probably never find a market.'

With tears welling up and my voice choking I let rip, 'You can get stuffed if you think I'll continue to play at your game, where my efforts increase and my returns are constantly diminishing,' and ran from the room, Paulz sitting stunned.

***

Jeremy and his Dad were responsible for a series of minor thefts across the district. Tools and small machinery from farm sheds, after cutting gate chains and padlocks and forcing other locks. Stuff stolen from sheds in town. Papers listed the thefts each month but no one came near guessing the thief.

When Jeremy did odd jobs he'd case the place returning months later to do his dirty business when memories had faded. Most bikes, ride-on mowers and machinery were still in his sheds, even receipts kept with them for the stuff they'd sold to secondhand dealers across the State.

We knew why he always had a dollar to spend.

The court kindly offered them a long free holiday inside the Geraldton Regional prison, all expenses paid.

CHAPTER FIFTEEN

Another one leaves

Secondary school loomed and everyone settled except me. Manju in Melbourne, Yonke Europe with her folks little to keep me. Boarding in Geraldton didn't appeal, Mingenew High a poor second without mates.

Yonke was given no notice of her parent's heading home. A great-aunt died leaving them wealthy. Great-aunt wanted Yonke to get a Degree in Amsterdam, so to get the qualifications she needed to finish school there. She didn't want to go but her parents were adamant. We spent a day hugging, crying and promising to keep in touch, for a while I thought she was going to miss Polo more than me.

Harry then Manju now Yonke.

Lost and bereft I became absolutely indecisive. For different reasons neither schooling option appealed. The local high attracted kids I had nothing in common with plus Jeremy's dead head mates went there. Geraldton meant boarding with strangers and trouble getting home weekends. No horse, no bike, no friends meant NO thank you.

That left my aunt in Victoria and a school bus. They were rellies that occasionally visited but were nice. Dad's older brother Bartholemew or Bart and his wife Doll, real name Agnes, were nice enough. It was easy to see why they chose their abbreviated names, with time and change of address everyone had forgotten their christened names.

The positives about their offer were it was nearer to Manju and I could ship over Yammy. Once settled someone would surely sell agistment for Dizzy. With Manju we might find a way to truck both horses across then maybe Yonke might send Polo over. A lot of maybes but better than none. Yonke might not stay with her parents, my aunt might be able to be convinced two teenagers was no worse than one, anything might happen and up until now in my life it usually had, so I agreed.

With all the carry on I almost forgot Harry, not even wondering if he was OK. I didn't feel guilty but in my heart but needed to hear.

Aunt Doll and Uncle Bart are both pretty fond of Harry, probably more than of me for all the standard reasons. He's a boy, quiet and handy. Well I could deal with the last two, they'd see I'd grown up since they last saw me and I reckoned I could show them I was pretty handy now. I was a country kid, I could deal with whatever.

CHAPTER SIXTEEN

Thank goodness for mobiles

Packing to leave home horse and room was traumatic, reminding me of leaving Warra. Living possessions tied me tightest. Mum and Dad would visit and keep in touch but Dizzy couldn't phone, my veggies wouldn't tell me what needed weeding and stock definitely wouldn't send reports. You can't hug a motor bike or kiss a ute goodbye, not while anyone was looking.

I didn't want the family to know I was upset.

Only days to go, it hit me. I'd completely forgotten Bop.

I had no idea why someone hadn't said something but I hadn't planned her into my shift. As the only good working dog on the farm since with the death of Buster the place couldn't operate without Bop's input.

Talk about a frantic series of discussions.

Everyone had an opinion.

Phoning elicited the response I could take her with me, but she'd need to be on the chain all day and no work was likely. There was no way I was going to allow that, she needed work and company. Uncle Bart suggested buying half a dozen old boners to run in the garden to keep Bop's eye in, Auntie Doll drew the line but had no better idea.

I became pretty tragic, my nights spent crying myself to sleep in despair. With no option but to stay on Walkaway, booking into one or other of the local High's, even if it meant bussing.

Finally a dream of Paulz with Bop at his heels. Next day I asked if he was up to looking after Bop.

With only a day to run through the commands Dad lent hand. Bop seemed relaxed when I handed her over to a new home, at Jamiesons out-camp. Arriving in Paulz' ute next day she jumped out, walking up as if nothing was new.

Another problem solved. On the second night Harry phoned, I never noticed the line didn't drop out. I found out much later that Mum had offered to pay him back, so he was on a land line not Skype. I didn't think of the cost or not being on Skype, I just needed to talk to him and hear his answer. He always had an answer to whatever.

***

Without discussion Mum and Dad had pre-empted my decision of school, quietly arranging things with Aunt Doll and Uncle Bart if my choice fell that way. Uncle Bart's Dad's brother but they never talk, which seems weird, even for adults. Mum keeps that side of the family link alive with phone calls and cards for birthdays and Xmas.

Their offer was cheap. I get on alright with them. I'd stayed so I knew my way around their house, the one tiny shop, closed-down pub and two plant nursery hamlet they call their village, so I decided.

***

Not that I was anxious or upset but so they remembered who I was, for longer than a week after I left home, maybe I did kiss everyone a hundred times. I especially gave Gran a hundred kisses so she remembered, ready to go she reached into her dressing gown, handing me a packet wrapped in pretty grey paper. 'Don't open it now, later will do, just a couple of things so you remember.'

***

Everyone told me there would be a few adjustments when I left home.

A few.

I expected a new diet, a new school uniform pretty was obvious up to a new teacher. New school rules, new friends, new school bus not unexpected.

But new climate.

No.

It was unseasonably cold for that time of the year. Cold I can handle but zero for days on end, snow one day, rain like always, fog so thick you could spread it on your sandwiches. New trees, new flowers on and on it went, every day something new.

Exciting but confronting. I'd decided not to go full of expectations, my experience was that way lay trouble. I only asked to have my own room with a bathroom, and space to have friends to sleep-over. The rest I would negotiate on the spot. Aunt Doll agreed easily so the decision was made.

The week before the school started Mum flew over to hand me across with much tear-shedding, asking Aunt Doll to drive us around the Bundowie school buildings so I'd know the landscape. The evening after Mum left Aunt Doll and Uncle Brad brought up their house rules. Stuff like meal times, tidiness, laundry (I did my own smalls), dish washing and bed times, what to call them at home and out with their friends. He was Unc anywhere, she was Aunt Doll outside and Auntie at home. If they served up something I didn't like just politely say so and it would not be on my plate again, though they might serve it to themselves. I told them I was fully house-trained, did not wet my bed, got up and went to bed early, knew how to wash dishes and was a bit of a neatness freak. It calmed any ragged nerves

Next day Aunt Doll drove me to the school, where she'd arranged for me to meet the Principal. Introduced himself with a warm handshake, 'David McKalister with a 'K' call me Headmaster or Mr Mac.'

He seemed OK, much younger than my primary school principal and pretty laid back without attempting to be 'cool'. Not a long talk, but reassuring.

'Any problems you can't sort drop by my office, no need for an appointment.'

To Aunt Doll's annoyance I carried my mobile everywhere, the dinner table was to be the exception. Another one, new family new rule, no calls at dinner, phone confiscated without exception. I took the chance of putting it on silent with a vibration.

Because I was too excited I blew it. The neighbours would have heard my squeal when I heard his voice. The phone was snatched away, not because it was at the table but when Aunt Doll heard my excitement she wanted first go, with Uncle Bart leaning over her shoulder once he woke up to who was calling. I instantly excused myself.

Harry finally said I need to talk to Fudge so Aunt Doll reluctantly handed the phone over, I less reluctantly left the room, headed to my own space and locked the door.

***

I didn't waste time when I got him to myself.

'You have no idea, I started. Nor do you! he continued.' It took several excited goes to calm down enough to get to grips with each other's news.

'Living here is different, school will be OK, some great kids and a really interesting teacher. Aunt Doll and Uncle Bart are the same as ever. I'd like to know why they never visit home but I'm scared to ask, given the skeletons we have.'

'Paulz's great, we caught Jeremy Davis stealing our field bins. Paulz soo cool in a crisis, Dad's will love him, Got him to buy a new wig so she looks better. You should have seen her deal with Jamie Douglas when she tried to jam me in the Coffee Palace. Totally dissed her, shut her straight out.'

I hardly drew breath with so much to sa, in a gap when I did draw breath Harry took over. 'You already told me most of that and it's nothing compared to my news.' So sure he was going to say they were going to get or had got engaged or Alysha was pregnant my brain wasn't fully engaged.

'I know the secret, you won't believe it, no wonder it's been a secret too dark to tell anyone of us. I didn't mean that as one of those double entry things, where you mean two things at once.'

'Dooble entedre, it's French and complicated, so you're forgiven, what do you mean dark secret and how did you find out.'

'Got sent into Wyndham to pick up stuff, the barge was late so we wandered along the main drag. A really old black stopped me, to bum a smoke. I didn't even look at him, you don't with bums up here, said 'I don't smoke and I'm too poor to give you one anyway.'

He stopped. Looked like he was drunk and wanted a fight so I backed off, said I don't want a fight mate and just walked away. He stayed looking at me then grabbed my shirt and stopped me dead.

'You must be old Harrold's boy, you're a dead spit of him, must be ninety by now.'

'Harrold who?' I asked, not thinking about 'old history' stuff while talking to an old black, I'd almost forgotten about Dad's caution.

'Don't get cheeky little white boy, your grand-daddy killed my sister after your daddy let her drown out in the Great Sandy.' He suddenly had a tight grip on my shirt front. I felt like belting him to get him off but I wanted to hear what he had to say, so I decided I could call the cops if it got too bad, meanwhile he just might have something we wanted.

'I don't know what you're talking about but I'll buy you a beer if you let go, otherwise I'll call the cops.'

He let go and headed to Wyndham's only hotel, The 'Town', with me and Angie in tow. Angie said later she was petrified I might get belted or finish in the lock up.

With a cold, frothy jug and two beer glasses between us plus a squash for Angie, sitting at an outside table his hangers on all told to 'p' off I poured him a cold schooner, froth on top fit for a king, while Angie drank from her schooner glass.

'OK so what's this all about. I never met you yet you reckon you know me. You say my granddad or my father killed your sister. Start talking or this'll be your last drink on me.' I bluffed.

He had a thick aboriginal accent so was hard to follow, but said he spotted the family resemblance straight off. reckoned I'm the dead spit of granddad, which we both know from the photos.

Then he got serious. Said back when the cattle lift was happening Dad had the hot's for his sister. She worked on the station and went along as camp cook following Dad.

Never came back.

We know one black girl didn't so it might be her.

'We've heard that blacks who came back told stories Dad could've saved her if he tried, I think that's why no-one ever talks about it, 'Old business' no more I think.' He finished.

I sat gob-smacked, silent, my brain hurting, with the implications and the long family silences. Though it made sense, but what would we do with it now we knew? I could hardly walk up to Dad and accuse him of falling in love with an Aboriginal, when it's so common today, also for allegedly not rescuing someone fifty years ago, Mum obviously knew yet she'd married Dad and kept the secret. Gran knew but she was closing down the memory factory, so it was hardly fair to her to ask, so I went on.

'I don't know what to do, it makes sense and you reckon he knew but what good is it now was it ever any good, is it our business? Maybe you should talk to Dad and see what he says happened.'

'No what we really need to do is find first-hand records of that whole business, a death like that must have been reported somewhere. You can't walk into the desert with a mob of cattle, then walk back months later, with people dead and missing, a mob of cattle lost, without reports somewhere.'

It'd never occurred to me before.

***

You wonder if someone from the CIA is listening when you Skype.

The line dropped out. Harry never called back, I kept getting an engaged signal.

I still hadn't told him about Bert and Lucy's money.

Stunned on the edge of my bed I tried making sense of what I'd been told, considering all I'd heard. Were poor decisions the only family failure.

Maybe something else was. But who knew and would tell. Did I have to go to the city library to find old papers.

CHAPTER SEVENTEEN

High school

Bundowie bus service collected me from the 'Trading Post' Mt Macedon's only food-shop, Post Office. A general meeting place for everyone.

I could be driven to College. It was only 5 kms over the hill, though Uncle Bart made it plain it wasn't part of their contract. After the farm, that was OK, I could always walk, if I could get Yammy over I could ride there, even without a license.

I didn't take account of the weather, which I found out quickly changed a dozen times a day, unlike home where what you put on in the morning was good all day. The walk downhill to the store took about ten minutes.

***

Mum left looking anxious and for the first fortnight called mobile after dinner every night. 'Not checking up, just wanted to make sure you have everything you need.'

'Like hello Mum, it's not like I'm living with strangers. Dad's family are my hosts they're both watching me like hawks and Uncle Bert's easier to talk with than Dad.

'Because he's not your father he doesn't have as many Dad things to consider, got me to thinking. I had to rethink a discussion over dinner. What I thought but didn't say was and they're probably reporting to you when I'm at school.

The first few days I was happy to hear a voice from home daily, it meant keeping up with how Bop was under the new arrangements, which generally calmed me.

A few nights after I arrived I found and opened Gran's packet. Most of the mountain heard my shriek of laughter. A packet of Meds, plus two packets of suppository contraceptives, with a yellow sticky note that read, 'Just in case' in Gran's inimitable copperplate hand.

Aunt Doll probably told the whole mountain after she calmed down. She'd burst into my room thinking I was being murdered, leaving laughing hilariously and repeating the story to anyone who'd listen.

***

About the time I left home I often felt tired without having actually done anything, which annoyed me, I'd always had heaps of energy but now sometimes felt washed out for days. Over the phone Mum said it was just more of what came with my package of hormones kicking in and arranged to start me taking a pretty evil-tasting iron supplement, to help ride the bumps. She packed three bottles.

***

I admit anxiety the first morning. I'd expected most kids would know each other from primary, sport or living locally. As everyone hung around on the wooden verandah of the Trading Post it seemed they'd met up over the holidays so just clicked back in. Looking awkward a bunch of us stood singly, in daggy, crisp, new uniforms, hoping for the ground to open before the College bus arrived. I was accidentally standing next to a spunk, who patently didn't want to talk or was too shy. The old hands seemed not to know him either, or else knowing he was the silent type so never included him. I began to doubt my choice of school, feeling well out of it all and uncomfortable, with niggling concerns over Bop.

Each new school year at home there were always those I knew, but minutes dragged, with me wondering if I'd chosen well. Still considering my future an old 80-seater bus swung in, right on time, a brown logo declared Dysons, nothing said Bundowie College, everyone headed to it, but in my state of mind it could have been collecting for the white slave trade.

Piling on I found myself sitting next to the spunk, he had the window to stare out and did. A girl I'd noticed and thought about trying to speak to was in the seat in front of me. She had the most stunning long lustrous hair, if she'd been my pony I'd have braided her thick brown mane. I hoped the trip was long enough so I could shift next to her.

While I considered the door closed. A kid standing in the middle of the bus loudly announcing. "Hi I'm Daniel, good to meet you all,' meeting cold silence.

Ignoring him and deciding everyone was on board the driver pulled away without warning. Bad luck if I'd been shifting seats.

A few k's down the hill the bus swung in to collect another bunch in matching uniforms. Again most knew someone.

Before the bus pulled back into the road, before it even started rolling forward the driver yanked the handbrake and stood up, blocking out half the light. He was huge with broad shoulders and pretty fat too. He did a good number in glaring at us all, one by one.

'Oi listen up you scruffy mob. I'm your driver all year, if you're lucky enough to pass then next year too. So let's get my rules straight. Do I have your undivided attention' As he was almost shouting and seats were packed we couldn't turn around. So it was fair to say he did, 'We'll get along just dandy if you do what I say. My rules aren't hard or easy but it's the way I like to run my bus, as he paused a bright spark down the back and put his two bobs worth in, 'If someone breaks a rule or two,' with no time to draw breath his answer thundered down the aisle.

'Everyone on the bus walks to school that morning Mr Smarty Pants, with you showing them the way. OK? '

Squirming his rump back into his seat he released the airbrakes, the bus slid away, in absolute silence as he was pulling into the school drive and no-one had spoken we still didn't know the rules. I figured he'd remember his oversight and tell us before we got off.

***

The fifteen minute drive to Bundowie College became an hour in isolation, despite several attempts to get a conversation going with my gorgeous neighbor I started nothing. He was either deaf, petrified, or seriously rude, the pony tail girl had been chattering earlier, but had also fallen silent. Scrambling to get off, impatiently slinging bags over shoulders, he blocked the door.

'Rule one! I make and I change the rules. Number two you mob do as I say. Number three keep the noise down to a roar. Rule Four sit tight in your seats and Five keep seat belts fastened, as you leave the bus please tell me your Christian name so I know who to shout at. See you at 3.45. Enjoy the year! '

With that he slid down the few steps to stand at the bottom where he shook hands with each giving our names. He looked us in the eye and simply said Call me Tiny.

Almost everyone headed directly to somewhere they seemed to know, taking the Principal at his word I headed to meet him. His secretaries, surprised said it wasn't usual.

She paused and apologised, 'I'm sorry I can't do it myself, someone will pick you up on Tuesday and show you around.' a lame offer after his offer of anytime I liked.

Wasn't I a bushie, so couldn't I find my own way around, heading for the nearest adult I asked directions. Didn't look much older than me but wasn't in uniform. QED a teacher.

Turned out he was, but was new too, but offered to show me to my room. He introduced himself as Steve, taught Phys Ed, said I'd meet him later and promptly got lost. Four other new kids wanted the Yr 8 class so fell in, following me using bush-craft to track down the room we needed.

***

The teacher in room 19 introduced herself as Claire, before asking us to give a one-minute wrap on ourselves. I was ready but the girl who'd looked at me earlier wasn't. She stood blushing scarlet, 'Angie!' beginning to talk, she stuttered so badly she was incomprehensible.

A boy I couldn't see down the back yelled out, 'Oh, hell, a stutterer what a year we'll have waiting for her brain to kick, half the class still laughing. I bounced out of my seat, spotted Mr Smartarse and walked right up to him. 'You've had your laugh, now you can apologise in front of us all, and while you're at it show us how smart you are at public speaking, in front of kids who don't know you!' Standing right in front of him I was daring him to try something clever.

He was pimply-faced, hadn't combed his hair, had his tie hanging loose, a splotch of last year's tomato sauce still on it. His face blushed red as I stared at him, like Poppa used to say most loudmouths are cowards, I wasn't backing down, if I had to live with him in class he could learn manners.

'We're all waiting, don't think anyone's going to laugh, apologise to Angie and make it sound like you mean it!' Looking at the floor he began to mutter, but not at the girl he'd offended. 'Look at Angie, act like the man you just might be when you're not being smart,' with that he lifted his head and quietly apologised. 'I'm sorry I was rude, it was stupid of me. I won't do it again.'

Angie smiled struggling to speak, 'Th-th-thank you, I acc accept your ap-ap-apology,' The class spontaneously clapped.

Walking to sit alongside her as Claire took the class back, trying to get us on track she ignored my outburst. 'Whose next, 'Phomn was Vietnamese an Australian child of refugees. 'Like Angie I too have a langrige problem, Engrish is not my first langrage. We speak Vietnamese at home, so I need more pwactice.' No one laughed.

Surprising me it was Daniel who chipped in, 'Hey I guess none of us speak Vietnamese, so you're one step ahead of us,' smiling at Angie.

The next kid was the real surprise package. The girl with the beautiful hair only looked confident because she was so gorgeous. When she stood up she spoke very quietly. 'I have a bad lithp and some ttt-times I stutter ttt-oo,' in a voice that seemed to come from far away. 'My name is SS-arah, I sometimes sign, to get round it,' and began signing.

The class was suddenly mute.

It was Mr Spunk who stood up. 'My name's Max, I might be able to interpret a bit. I got a Court order for being drunk in public and finished up working in a place for speech-impaired people. It's not that good-a-story but I'd like to help, to make up for being rude. I can sign slowly.'

I began to think Mt Macedon was where all the naughty kids had got sent.

***

Embarrassing for everyone. Sure I wasn't the only thinking Claire should've known about Sarah's problem and the school should have arranged for a signer to help, brain still in low gear I stood without really thinking and blurted.

'I think it's disappointing the school isn't more supportive to us new kids.' In the pause Max collected his stuff, shifting to the empty chair alongside Sarah's desk, not quite knowing how it would help, but wanting to express solidarity. She smiled quickly passing a note and mouthing thanks.

By mid-morning everyone had been through the inquisition, tension had eased, some kids knew where the tuck shop was so we headed there. Sarah carried a pad and I realised how much she depended on a quick hand to be included. She wrote a second note 'U wre brave, could teach U 2 sign 'f U want'

'I want,' smiling into the diminishing space between us, responding to her smile I answered. 'Nana always said in Australia they don't hang you for speaking up, and silence is never golden when someone's in bother.'

Sarah smiled back 'Can talk a bit, sounds weird, couldn't talk proply, folks sent me 2 school 4 deaf n mute kids, learned 2 sign fast didn't speak much.' she quickly scrawled.

So would you rather talk or sign? I asked. 'I reckon I can learn to understand you either way I'm a quick learner.'

'Bit f both f I can,' she wrote as we headed back to class, Max caught up as we walked in. 'Hope I didn't make things worse back there,'

'You w w were brave,' Sarah murmured, smiling a brilliant grin.

***

'Should I tell Claire or will you,'

'f you c-c-could it'd be q-q-quicker.

I did.

Before everyone sat I brought Claire up to date, apologising for being abrupt and speaking out of turn. The class fell silent waiting.

'No it's really my fault,' she replied turning to the class, 'I was at fault, this is my first class so I'm probably as nervous as some of you.' The whole class looked amazed, she was obviously about thirty.

'I was a late starter as a teacher. I did a Law degree, working as a lawyer before I retrained as a teacher. This is my second career, but importantly it's the career I chose and not my parents.' That one line started our love affair with Claire.

Within minutes the whole class was asking questions. Everyone turned out to be concerned about career choices, coming to a small rural High school had brought the issue into sharp focus. Some felt under pressure from parents or family, some had no idea or leads, everyone was busting to understand what work outside of home or casual jobs was really like, almost none of us had older siblings employed off the land.

Open, honest, willing to talk about her work career and family background, Claire instantly connected. A country girl she'd shifted to the city to study and work, I easily related to her, others grew up in outer suburbs or their parents shifted to rural communities to afford houses, and in the shifts kids lost connections, leaving them at odds and ends. In Claire's story we discussed finding connections.

By lunch break most heard stories like them.

Over lunch Max joined Angie, Sarah, Phomn and of all people Daniel who followed Angie, finding a spot we began sorting stuff over a sandwich, by break end we had a better picture of each other. We all lived pretty close and shared some interests so before heading back to room 19 we decided to chat further on the afternoon bus.

The afternoon passed quickly, a vibrant buzz through the class, picking up on it Claire chatted easily about options for study programs over the coming term, explaining the curriculum. We understood better what she had to achieve and how there was more than one way to complete our year's work. When she explained 'Lessons can be designed to fit in with your interests and school didn't have to be boring', she gained our attention. We discovered she'd been to an Alternative school, so didn't see the education process in the same way as most.

'If the class agrees to work together I'll redesign our year's work those in favour,' Every hand shot up.

'OK that's a wrap, your bus'll be ready, no homework, see you all tomorrow, think of projects.'

And we were gone.

On board the bus phone numbers, address and family names were swapped, so parents or carer's could get involved, everyone agreeing to be early at the Trading Post till we could do an overnight at someone's house.

First question when I walked in was as expected, 'Have a good day,' they were surprised when after only one day at school I asked. 'Do you know the families of any of my new friends, here's a list of their names. We want to arrange a sleep-over for five kids as soon as we can, we have an assignment on critical thinking and will need space to work'

Unc took me into his library.

With a sweep of his hand he indicated four walls covered in books, with a huge central oak table and a smaller writing desk to one-side. 'This is our critical thinking room, there are the resources and the writing space. You are all welcome to use anything in the room.'

I gazed in absolute awe, except in movies or in magazines I'd never seen such a place in a house.

'Wow where do we start,'

'What question do you want to answer most,'

It's strange but at that instant Harry's question shot up, school work forgotten.

'Have you got reports of what happened when the cattle got lost'

I swear he blanched a bit, but then walked to a ladder and slid it to the centre of the floor to ceiling set of shelves and climbed up.

'Your Mum warned us you're just like your Granddad. No beating around the bush something to say, out it comes, straight to the point.'

Climbing down he carried a well worn leather-bound journal, what he said took my breath away in a moment.

'These are the newspapers of the day, they report it all including the Coronial Court and the verdict reached. I'll leave you to it and see you for dinner seven sharp, it's a roast.'

That was at five o'clock.

He collected me at seven.

I hadn't moved, just kept reading the hundreds of pages from front to back.

Aunt Doll smiled as she laid a huge plate full of roast veggies in front of me, over it was a thick slurp of gravy running to the edge of the plate.

'Your Mum described this as your favourite meal, I thought we would start with it and go downhill from there!'

Surprise after surprise. What else had they talked about.

They had their meat and I could see more veggies in a warmer should I manage to come back for seconds. I could have but didn't do an Auntie Merle and wipe the plate with my finger either, nor do a big belch. I attacked it with gusto, unaware of the silence.

'Awesome Aunt Doll, Mum said you were the better cook but this is amazing and huge and unexpected. Thank you very much but you don't need to keep it up or I will stack on weight.'

She smiled at Unc, swung toward me, reached for my hand and with no sense of an admonition went on, 'We usually say grace before we eat, but you seemed so hungry it would have been a shame to interrupt you. Perhaps we can give thanks.'

I was embarrassed by my lack of manners, we never say grace at home, I'd been told they did and completely forgot.

Thanks were simple.

'We give you thanks Lord for our new house guest and for the food you have blessed our table with and ask you to put food on the tables of all those less fortunate. Amen.'

Talk about a heathen. I felt unchristian rude and plain bad mannered and awful for pigging in when such good food had been specially prepared for me.

It was not the best of first impressions.

With extraordinary grace Aunt Doll smiled, seeking to minimise my embarrassment,

We should have warned you that we say grace when we talked about house rules. We know your family don't but it's our way of thanking the Lord for the abundance of our life. We do it for every meal but otherwise we are not church goers or bible bashers.'

Unc smiled, 'At least you didn't do a Merle and wipe your plate clean with your fingers, now if you have ever seen it, that is embarrassing'.

It gave me an out and an opening so I recounted her last visit and our embarrassment.

'So did you find anything interesting,' Unc opened to help cover my embarrassment. 'It would be pointless to say you have no idea what I found, because I can tell from how worn the papers are that someone has read the print off them. Any chance it was you.

He smiled a droll grin and turned to Aunt Doll, 'We thought you might find interesting stuff in there.'

They'd beaten me there!

'Do you also know what happened to the fortune that Gran lost and what it is about the pearler she mumbles on about.'

Uncle Bart sighed, sounding deeply hurt, as if I had lanced a much more painful set of memories this time.

'I can show you the letters from the solicitors and a Court record of when we tried to recover it. Gran was foolish, some would say stupid, others might say love struck, but she got no warranty or security for a single dollar she'd lent, and told no-one at home. The same storm that struck the cattle wiped out most of the pearl fleet, which unknown to us our money had been spent on.'

He almost glared down the table at no one.

'Bloody man, a real opportunist, just boarded a boat and sailed away. As far as we know he never came back, never apologised, never wrote to Gran and lived his days out in Paris, with his real wife.'

I seemed to be spending my time catching up on who was who and who did what, then working out where to put all the new information into my mental filling cabinet, before the next question popped up.

This one popped up out of left field, 'So is that what you argued with Dad about.'

Uncle Bart and Aunt Dot both changed posture, exchanging a long glance across the table, 'It's one of many things, most of which are better left buried, we have no way of ever healing some of the words we both shouted. Those wounds still fester, so to let them die I don't raise that with others anymore. You'll not get anything more from me about it, so best let that be.' I could hear a sharp edge that had crept into his voice.

Looking across at Aunt Doll for support she gently shook her head, 'Just let them all die. No good will ever be served raising any of them. We've all moved on and you need to. Even though you might want to know, unless you want to end up like the others let it go. Your Dad can't and poor Gran is just suck in limbo unable to set herself free of her own stupidity. When she dies the whole sorry mess can die with her.'

She did a Mum, walking out to the stove to make a cuppa, while Unc did a Dad and buried his face in the local paper.

Thanking them I got up and did it myself, going back into the library to pick up a volume of old papers, before returning to sit silently until I decided to go to bed.

I walked over to Unc to kiss his head, 'I'm sorry Unc I had no idea, but I'll let it go and thanks for being so open. I'll tell Harry as well.'

Walking toward Aunt Doll's chair Uncle Bart began to speak behind me, with his mouth full of a piece of chocolate.

After starting with, 'Your Mum mentioned old Bert had left you alright,' he choked, which led to Aunt Doll chipping him again, 'Bart please don't talk with your mouth full, apart from almost choking there's a child watching and its bad manners.'

With little more than a nod of an apology in her general direction he cleared the blockage with some cold tea and went on, 'She raised it with me because she reckons I've managed our money from the break up better than most. She thought I might be able to help you decide how to manage Bert's bonanza.' He stopped and looked at Aunt Doll, turning to look at me almost as an aside. He continued, 'I can't say I'm certain it couldn't have been done better, but the way we did it gave both of us a real chance to pursue our dreams. We paid our way through Uni to take PHd's in the areas we were fascinated with, not even considering what help it might make to a lifetime career. We weren't able to live like royalty, but neither did we need to work as cleaners like other students. We were able to take holiday breaks when they came. Being a mature age student at Uni can be pretty hard if you have no money or parents to sub you.'

Shocked, embarrassed and annoyed that Mum hadn't discussed her talking to Uncle Bart about me I was somehow relieved too. The deaths and the money had come too suddenly, in a space too crowded by other stuff. Apart from a string of nights when I had weird dreams I'd put down to sleeping too hot, I'd put the whole issue in the back of my mind after Dad's brief comment, always with a niggling feeling I should grow up. I felt I needed to take control and be more responsible about such a windfall, not leave it to Dad although I thought he was safer than some lawyer I'd never met. Too often I saw newspaper articles about lawyers who stole trust funds.

Dad seemed safer.

***

With no hard idea until now how Uncle Bart spent his share of the division of the property money I'd not given it much air, without knowing I supposed he'd just lived it up.

***

We retired to the library. Aunt offered to bring in a pot and she disappeared.

He was sitting across the big reading table, the other side from where I'd sat earlier that night discovering the old business. It felt there was some residual special energy in the air, after opening a piece of long silent family history Unc opened the air.

'If anything was possible what would you do, what would be the things you'd want. Don't stop to think rationally, just let rip about the dreams you said you had.'

Embarrassed to tell an adult I looked down at the table, 'I dreamt of a jaccuzi on the verandah, no water just full of Smarties, jelly beans and ice cream.'

He didn't snigger or chuckle, I looked up to see him not even grinning.

'Pretty standard kid stuff, but not the sort of investment you might need to sustain you later in life.'

I took it up again, 'Mostly I really want to show Dad I can run Walkaway but I'm not going to pay to buy that right from him. I'd rather go north, teaming up with Harry somewhere.' Blushing I went on, 'No matter what I do Dad can't see me as capable as I know I am.'

Taking a long breath Uncle Bart looked directly at me, 'Where would you go with Harry, what sort of place do you think you both want to buy?'

He took a deep breath again, 'Between you there's something like two million dollars, that's a lot of options!'

Placing a sheet of paper on the table he drew columns before he looked at me again, let's list some options as he leant back. He wrote nothing, I found it amazingly difficult to write a word.

'Perhaps if I start.'

How differently he saw the opportunities Bert's passing had left us. I knew Bert and Lucy's gifts offered us multiple futures, but hadn't settled down to map them out. My dreams were full of horses, horse floats, bigger better bikes and a trip to see Yonke with Manju paid to come too. All pretty incidental when I listened to his way of seeing it. I quickly became a grown-up instantly apparent none of my dreams were for the long term. I scanned his columns headings.

Education. Work choices. Your own family. Location.

'So what is your biggest dream, what does Harry want with his life and has that not so little quiet as a church mouse sister ever talked about what she wants to make of her life.'

As I didn't answer he continued, 'Have you talked to each other or thought about doing something together. Forget the way your own family have lived such fractured lives. You each now have a chance to write a brand new page or even a book entirely of your own.

I realised I hadn't talked to Sis, it had all happened so fast I hadn't even discussed it with Harry just assumed what he might want and couldn't even guess what sis might want. Bert died, Lucy came and went, school started and suddenly my life was traveling at a gallop, in completely new directions.

We broke up after an hour of talking, I went to bed and waited and waited and waited.

Aunt Dot came in to kiss me goodnight, she looked down, smiling, 'Your Dad may call it The Old Business, but he can't let it go. It's going to be up to you and Harry now, your Dad had to be dragged to Court to get back the money he owed Uncle Bart, so Bart's never trusted him with money since, he thinks he might have the same problem Gran had back then.' She looked down conspiratorially.

' Don't tell him I told you but that's why Bart thinks you should get control of it yourself, not put temptation in front of your father. You sleep on it . Night nite.'

I thought and thought and thought, about how it all fitted together, until sleep twisted my nose and dreams grabbed me leaving me with no answer but a clear line of thinking to get around to.

CHAPTER EIGHTEEN

The first few weeks

'We now know the class is made up of a few country kids and a heap of city kids, to me that's not a problem, it actually provides a perfect opportunity to create real knowledge. I'm not into just reading books, I'm a strong believer real learning happens through experience' Claire opened.

We stopped clattering chairs, then class began to chatter, in a minute no-one was listening either to each other or to Claire, she had to shout to be heard over the din. 'Quiet please everyone, let's not get over-excited, it won't mean you don't have to study, you'll still need to read, but you'll learn to read critically, co-operatively, and on interesting topics, instead of just set texts. You'll do your work researching in the school library and on-line, using the internet's resource library. I promise you it will NOT be an easy option but I also promise it WILL be fun.'

I was amazed to see how suddenly she was in control and in a couple of seconds had everyone listening. 'I was taught to learn to see every obstacle as an opportunity, each problem as a chance to solve something, so as the class solves each problem we all learn, we learn to co-operate and do deep research, not just skim the surface, but look critically at each piece of information we find.'

Class hero put her hand up to get attention, 'I have two questions please, don't you need to get permission from someone and what do we call you, Teacher, Mrs something or Claire.'

Before she could reply Mr Smarty Pants butted in, 'and what's critical thinking does that mean objecting to everything or what and what if someone's on my team that I don't like much,'

'All good questions, but one thing at a time,' she glared back. 'Jim I expect everyone to put their hand up like Kimberley, and wait to be asked not just yell out. It's good manners and a way to ensure everyone gets a go. Is that understood'

'Yes Miss', apologetically.

'While we're on the subject, can I make it clear how I'd like the classroom to operate? Jim's clarified rule one, my second is one person speaking at a time, my third I expect everyone to behave like adults, and lastly, No swearing in class or outside. Any problems with any of those rules.'

Not a murmur, 'Ok to answer your questions I do have to get the Principal's approval. I don't envisage problems if I present a sound case with projects to support my program. You call me Miss Collins, I call you by your Christian names.'

Looking directly at Daniel she answered in a serious tone, 'That's one good question Daniel, keep them up. Critical thinking is another way of seeing both information and the world. It's as old as civilsation, but as new as tomorrow. We will do several lessons and a test to see if everyone has understood the concept before we move forward.'

***

I sat up front to look carefully at Tiny,as I clambered off I turned.

'I reckon you're probably not a meanie, just a careful driver,' ducking my head before he could respond.

CHAPTER NINETEEN

Day Two, Critical thinking

The day's lesson was Critical Thinking, a topic I was still mulling over with what I now knew from Unc and Harry, wondering how to think critically about the issues raised. Seems everyone thought I'd be leading from the front but to everyone's dismay I was mute, walking directly to Room 19 with my entourage, all noisily finding seats when Claire came in and grabbed our full attention.

Dressed in a colourful peasant style blouse, embroidered patterns down the edges of the button-hole seams, she also wore hand tooled cowboy boots.

We were all eyes. Her faded jeans were stuffed into the vintage calf length cowboy boots.

No one said a word, all of us just stared, with fly-caching mouths, no primary school teacher had ever arrived dressed in this sort of gear. Her brown shoulder length hair hung loose, brushed out and straight. It shone, a genuine hippie straight out of the magazines. Taking no notice of our slack-mouthed stares, she just started class.

'A few hundred thousand years ago cavemen walking out of caves began clustering in mud huts, which slowly grew into villages, quickly evolving into cities. Probably since the first mud hut agglomerate formed, those residents felt themselves superior to country folk.'

She broke our stares by continuing, 'Later wealthy folk living in the cities longed to escape the smog and density associated with stressful city living, those who were financially able began heading back, building large country estates.'

That rang bells somewhere although we hadn't considered ourselves part of a historic population drift. No-one commented or asked questions.

'These days people are moving out of city houses, into country housing estates, so far as I know no-one's begun a movement back to caves, although some adventurous souls do build houses into the sides of hills.'

With no interruptions she asked a question.

'Have I lost you or are you finding it a bit daunting.'

Max spoke, 'No it's cool we're just not used to being asked to set our own work and thought today would be about critical thinking.'

She smiled a real hippy grin across her face, 'I'd like to suggest the topic for our first project. As a learning and research process and to weld the class together we might critically examine the urban / country divide, as represented in this class.'

Looking at a sea of slightly uncomprehending faces she asked, 'All OK on that.'

Again we sat mute, we could break into three groups, one of all country kids, one all city kids and the third kids from families who've been around the area for a few years longer than most. Still no real movement but a lot of chatter as we tried to work out what group we belonged to. Claire didn't seem fazed by our lack of action so went straight on. 'This won't be the only project we undertake, I'd be keen for the class to have perhaps three different projects running simultaneously. Choosing different teams for each project will stretch your minds, as well as opening you up rapidly to knowing everyone in the class and the community.'

When no one moved she went around the class breaking us into the groups she'd already decided on. She listed our names and told us she would print a schedule of who was in which group. Group One included Kimberley, Max, Sarah. Group Two was Daniel, Lauren, Phong and Group Three was Me, Angie and a kid who had said nothing Trevor. There were others to fill numbers but no-one I knew then.

'One thing I've noticed as you all explain yourselves is that you each see a genuine divide between city and country people and the way they live. I agree with you. If you'll work with me we can set up projects that each of you can get involved in. That will be where we get our lesson material from, this will be how we learnt to think critically. Away you go, we'll break at lunchtime and see where we get to.' Dragging a couple of tables together we sat looking at each other.

OK who wants to start' I asked as everyone seemed to be looking at me.

'Can we set a few rules so Angie is fully with us' no-one demurred so on I went 'Class rule two beats rule one,' Angie put her hand up. 'C-C-Can we take notes s-s-so we all have s-s-something to f-f-fall back on, I w-w-will keep a record I can write fast.' Everyone had thought they would have to, so Angie was elected instantly recorder. I took the floor again, 'Can I suggest we challenge the statement even before we start, that's supposed to be part of critical thinking and challenge the assumptions, 'just as the class door opened.

CHAPTER TWENTY

The Universe unfolds as it should

For days in both the front and back of my mind I was worrying about how to deal with Harry's news, so wasn't really focused on the money thing.

Then Miss Collins called me to the Principal's office. I thought it would be my day dreaming, something I'd done on the bus, or my attitude in class.

'Hello Kimberley,' as polite as ever.' I have a request from your mother to let you go home.'

'Have I done something wrong'

'No, it's your grandmother. She's had a bit of a turn and wants to see you. Your mother has booked you on the first flight back to Perth, where she will meet you. You're excused from class for a week. Mrs Collins may set you some work.'

I knew Gran wasn't well, we'd all watched and heard her becoming more vague and losing her appetite for months, the morning I left she came down in her dressing gown to see me off. Taking me aside she whispered her confidence, 'I am very proud of you, you remind me of myself as a child. I expect great things from you,' then slipped back into dreaming and stood singing an old lullaby before asking 'if you'll pick me a billy of blackberries I'll make you some of my special hot jam to put on your eggs at school.'

I'd promised I'd pick some later and suddenly felt there may not be any 'later'. I now stood feeling a long way from home in Mr David McKalister with a K's suddenly cold office, my hot tears welling up and spilling down my cheeks despite trying to be brave. Gran was the last of my super special people since Poppa died, and I was not ready to let her go just yet. I had hoped to come home from school covered in the glory of some special prize, to make her proud in lieu of Poppa.

***

Harry's call came through as I waited at Tullamarine airport.

'When do you land Sis? I get in at two Mum's picking me up Alysha's coming down with me we're going to tell the folks. Do you know how crook Gran is.'

'No idea. I get in at one thirty but while I have you Bert and Lucy left you a heap. You are rich brother,' and the CIA intercepted us again.

***

I really had no idea how bad Gran was but figured Mum wouldn't have called us both back if it wasn't serious. I'd tried to get through but the line was constantly engaged. Harry's flight was due to land half an hour after mine, so I guessed Mum had arranged it so she didn't have to wait around and could get home quickly.

'How was Gran when you left' as I gave her a huge hug while she rushed me out of the airport waiting area. She grabbed my small overhead locker case and marched me out to the car, not saying a word except to return my hug. Anyone could see she'd been, and was still almost crying. I knew she'd have been driving for at least two hours, so must be very tired, especially if she'd been sitting up with Gran for a night or two.

'She's not well at all. Two small strokes left her with a bit less speech and total paralysis down one side. But she made it clear she wanted to see you both so here you are. You'll see her face has sagged even further and she can't walk at all. The doctor says she may not survive another one and it could happen anytime. Dad's struggling with it. You'll see when we get home.'

I was standing next to her, holding her hand in the baggage collection area as we saw Harry walking toward us, hand in hand with Alysha. She was much darker skinned than I remembered from school and twice as gorgeous.

I felt Mum's grip tighten.

'That's Alysha Mum, you might remember her from school,' and Harry was on us before I could explain.

'Mum this is my fiancé Alysha, she will be staying with us, in my old room.'

A statement not a question.

Harry had a new found confidence.

He gave Mum his usual big hug and smiled at me over her shoulder.

It was one of those moments when you hold your breath wondering if you know what will happen next.

'Of course, you studied French together. Your family were refugees from Uganda, but you went to school in England didn't you. As I recall you managed to scrape this son of mine through his oral, but despite your help he didn't quite manage the written. Welcome to the family.'

I felt a swelling of pride in my throat and hoped Dad would perform as well. For the drive home Mum asked Alysha to sit in the front and engaged her, while Harry and I caught up in the back. I reckoned she thought Alysha would have been easier to pump than Harry. I kept catching fragments of their conversation and knew Harry was listening hard as well.

'So how are your parents, has your father found constant work these days? I think he was going back to do a refresher course when I last heard.'

Alysha's soft voice was so not audible in the back that I felt like leaning over and asking if she could turn the volume up.

'So you two bumped into each other up north?' I knew she wouldn't be able to wait.

Harry ran flank immediately, 'No Mum, I picked Alysha up from Manjimup where she was living. She's been with me since I left home. We both work out on El Questro. You and Dad should come visit us. It's the most amazing place but expensive unless you camp. Every day it's so beautiful it takes our breath away.' He didn't leave Alysha out to dry for a second.

As always Mum was quick on the uptake, 'What job have you each got?' looking over her shoulder at Harry.

'I'm Manager of maintenance, in charge of four staff, all repairs and grounds, not bad for the son of a cocky eh. That's why I never have time to write. No mobile reception there so no calls home! But we love it and everyone gets on really well. Alysha's in charge of a team of cleaners and rooms,' his voice glowing with pride at her rank.

I couldn't hear much over the engine and road noise but figured Mum would continue to pump Alysha about what she did, where they lived, what their diet was and whether her little boy was being looked after properly.

Harry began by telling me excitedly about the bigness of the Kimberley. 'It's not like here, up there you look up into a baby blue sky, day after day. It's somehow wider and deeper and the horizons seem further apart too. The jets to Asia fly over most days, so high there's no sound from them so you look up seeing an invisible pilot in a silver dot, trying to doodle a giant graffiti straight line across a clean page, while his primary school teacher isn't watching. What starts out as a straight line across that page becomes a lazy set of wiggles that eventually dissolves into a vast silent pale blue sky-scape.'

His travelogue slowed as he stared into some space in his mind. It was obvious something about the place had deeply affected him.

I took my turn and told him about Paulz, the way he operated and what fun he was to work with, making it plain he wasn't abnormal, but looked different somehow. I was filling him in on catching Jeremy and using the header to cover the heap when

I remembered the money, which I really hadn't even addressed properly since talking with Unc. 'Bert left you and me and Sis everything, and then Lucy left him all her houses, so they come to us too. Each of us is probably worth about a million dollars. I don't really know exactly how much, but Bert left us heaps and from what Lucy left there was obviously good money when she was working the game and later with her husband an accountant she bought houses. She ran a home for wayward girls too. It's waiting in a lawyer's bank account, or else Dad has it somewhere. I'm going to get my share out and manage it myself. I'll tell you why later but you and sis should do the same.'

I'd hardly got on a roll and did not want to talk about it with Mum in the front seat with her big ears, before we had to stop for fuel. It was probably just as well for Alysha, she must have felt like a victim of the Spanish Inquisition by the time Harry and she changed places.

He'd only just begun telling me about the old black-fellow as Mum pulled into the servo.Talking with Alysha was easy, she was full of funny stories about El

Questro and the dudes they worked with. I knew she'd fit in at home once we teamed up to jump the hurdle of Dad. I also knew Harry and I needed to find some time alone, or maybe with Alysha, but not with parents

CHAPTER TWENTY-ONE

Harry the hurdler

There was no way Mum could have warned Dad, so Alysha would be a straight-out test of his attitudes. The last time I knew he'd worked or mixed with anyone as black as Alysha was as a kid in the Kimberley. We hardly had an Aboriginal in the Shire, and none had worked for us as casuals. Alysha looked as if she could be a mixed blood Aboriginal, like some of the beautiful mixed blood people from around Broome, despite or perhaps because her Ugandan heritage.

Dad met the car as Mum parked it on the curved drive in front of the house.

He almost rushed Harry, I'd never seen them give each other such a hug.

Still getting the bags out of the boot I heard the click as the rear door as it opened and turned to watch. Mum was only halfway across to Dad when Alysha stepped out, on the side nearest to the house. Even from where I was I swear I could hear Dad's sudden intake of breath. I froze thinking all hell was about to explode, it sounded the same as the noise he makes when he's really angry.

I held mine and I'm sure Harry held his breath as he broke from the hug, extended his hand for a handshake and introduced Alysha. 'Dad, I'd like to introduce my fiancé Alysha,' and paused, 'We got engaged a few days ago.' I could hear the shivering combination of pride and nervousness in his voice.

Dad's face contorted into a series of shapes I'd never seen before, he stared, seemed to frown quizzically, then his face erupted in a vast smile, and he held both hands out to gently hold and shake Alysha's.

She never hesitated but stepped in closer to hug him, her arms wrapping as far around his back as they could reach. 'Hello Dad.'

'Welcome to the family and Walkaway,' he growled in his usual deep voice, belied by the smile spreading all over his grey whiskery face, which he might have shaved if he'd known he had a visitor coming.

I'm sure Harry was as shocked and pleased as I was, I had no idea where such a reaction had come from or what it meant.

***

Gran was sitting hunched over in front of a roaring fire, rugged up in her wheelchair, her un-brushed thin wispy hair all over the place, she lifted her head unsteadily before she too stared at Alysha.

'It's Alice, isn't it,' she stuttered as she beamed.

Like Harry; I thought she was just confused. Then I thought no, Gran would never have met Alysha when she was at school with Harry.

'No Gran this is my fiancé Alysha. We got engaged up north,' Harry explained quietly.

Gran searched Alysha's face, looked at Harry then searched the room for Dad, 'She looks just like Alice. I thought she must still be alive, but that was too long ago wasn't it or am I just confused.' she inquired of Dad as he walked closer to be in her focus.

***

Mum bustled in with her usual tray of cups teapot and buttered scones. 'This might be the time Brad, you'll never get a better one,' she gently admonished.

He sighed, sagged, then straightened himself, before he took a brimfull cuppa and walked to stand close beside Gran's wheelchair.

'Mum' he started gently 'You are right Alice is still dead. She died on the trip out into the desert all those years ago, you remembered it right. This is Harry's new lady, her name is Alysha, amazingly like Alice in name and looks, so it's easy to be confused. They've got engaged.'

A lifetime of grief and pain was exhaled in a single long breath.

'Alice and I never did.'

'Oh!' was all Gran whispered, as she stared from face to face, struggling to make the damaged gears in her rusty brain engage. I walked over to hold her hand, kneeling next to her, opposite Dad. She refocused to look at me.

'Hello Gran, its Kimberley. I came back from my new school. You remember I went to High School near Aunt Doll and Uncle Brad. I live with them now. I'm doing all right, but I heard you were a bit crook so I flew back.'

'Yes, but Brad doesn't like me much anymore, he never drops in for visits.'

She wheezed and coughed as she stared hard at me. 'I think I've had that turn you told me not to, Doc says I might not be around for your graduation,' without a hint of self pity.

Harry knelt in front of Dad, on her other side, reaching for her spare hand, his voice confident yet soft, 'It's Harry Gran,' as she swiveled her face to find the source he went on, 'Well darling it looks like the Old History has finally surfaced, without anyone having to be hung, to get it out of you all.'

She may have been struck with a couple of huge strokes but enough of Gran's face and mind still worked, she cracked a lopsided smile.

'I'm sorry that I am so tired so very tired, but how lovely she looks.' Again she searched for the face she wanted. 'Alice did too, but you know back then white men and black girls didn't mix in polite company. Such a pity Bradley did love her, we all knew' her voice audibly weakening as she talked. As she ended the sentence she slowly slumped forward, snoring as she slept.

***

I hadn't noticed Dad sneak out, until he reappeared with one of the oldest framed photos from the hall. 'I don't know who is the more beautiful. I was in love with one so I'm biased. You can make your own comparisons, because there she is in the background of the shot taken as we headed into the desert.' His face looked wrought and his eyes reached to mine for understanding.

'It's quite alright.' Mum murmured, returning my glance to her for some sort of support. 'Your Dad told me the whole story long before I married him. I've watched Alice checking me out each time I walk down the hall. We're old friends now. That was all so long ago.'

'So what is the whole story Dad, can you tell us or is it too hard.' Harry asked gently, standing up from Gran's side.

'Well it used to be, but it doesn't all seem so hard now, something about the way that you've got engaged to Alysha and ...' he waited until he drained his cup and looked across at Mum, and down to Gran before he spoke again, 'It's two lifetimes ago and things were different then. Like Mum says, White men never married Aboriginal girls. Black girls were below them, even looking at one was frowned on and Alice was our kitchen hand, so just a servant. I used to help her peel the spuds. '

'That's how I knew,' piped up Gran, who must have been still listening despite the appearance of sleeping, 'I saw you giving her moon eyes when I burst in one day without knocking.'

I presume giving someone a moon eye was not quite the same then as a brown eye is now Harry cheekily asked, and after a glare from Mum was left to wonder. Dad simply ignored him as he sat on the edge of his armchair.

'When my father wanted a cook for the trip Alice put her hand up. She was taken because Mum said she could go, a last minute thing, a terribly fateful thing,' he sighed as he stared down at the picture now in his lap and continued.

'Each evening it took a couple of riders to settle the mob down for the night, no portable fences back then, just a good open spot, someone riding and crooning them down to sleep. We all took turns, Alice and I managed to take turns the same nights. I don't think anyone noticed until the storm came. That day's drove had ended near a dry wash which Dad thought was just the spot to bed them down. Clean, dry sand, shaded high banks so we made camp on top of the banks, looking down at the mob.

You could see he was remembering as he stared into some place none of us could visit with him. Alysha quietly took the photo-frame from him and began to study it glancing around the room.

'Bad decision, maybe a day before, a hundred miles away, a cyclone had dumped a billion gallons on the catchment area. We didn't even know there was a blow in the area, no radio then, no weather forecast, we could just see a set of distant storm cloud on the edge of the horizon.

Again his stare drifting away.

A'lice and I'd arranged to take someone else's turn, so we were on duty for the second night in a row. We'd drop-tied our horses up on the bank, away from the camp, we'd taken our boots off and were chasing each other around the sand, naked as babies, a hundred yards down creek from the mob. We were being quiet, having a lovely time when we heard the change in the tone of the mob. We didn't need to talk, we knew the sound of the mob stirring, but not why. Running in thin moonlight, we couldn't find our boots and clothes quickly.'

He was gasping for breath 'The mob came crashing down on us, we later found out they were spooked by the silent waters, appearing at increasing speed, getting deeper by the second in the previously dry bed.' He choked up as Mum moved to him and put her arm around his shoulder.

'It seems so childish and silly now. Dad should never have camped the mob in a dry creek, Alice and I shouldn't have been fooling around and Dad shouldn't have drunk

the bottle of rum, chaos, total flaming chaos, pitch bloody black, noisy as hell, I was grabbing my trousers and boots when I glimpsed Alice, with her smock on running for the bank... then I guess a steer hit me. Then the mob was on us both. I woke up when the water hit my face, clambered dizzily up the bank to find my horse, but Alice's was gone. My first thoughts were to head the mob off, our fortunes were locked up in them, I had no idea where anyone else was. I was so sure Alice had made it up the bank to her horse, she was such a good stockman. It wasn't until about mid-day when we all found ourselves back at the camp, each with a handful of frightened stragglers, that I went to find her.'

***

He got up heading to the loo, while Mum boiled another kettle and made a fresh pot. Dad came back in his face wet and took the offered cup. He smiled softly at Mum before he took a sip and spoke into the mystery.

'She was trampled to death, not a pretty sight except her face, it didn't have a mark on it. We buried her out there, under a gimlet tree. Old Paperbark himself told us what to do. He was a top law man and her proper uncle. He sang the song lines and spoke some words in language so her spirit would know where to go. He died on the long walk home, no injuries we knew of. But an old man, and he grieved over Alice. So when we finally got back with under two hundred cattle left of the mob we walked out with, the stories started. I couldn't admit to loving Alice and being naked in the creek with her. Paperbark knew but he had died a day later, and we buried him next to her so I got the blame. Blackfellas always had to pin it on someone or some spirit. So I took it, if I'd followed custom and common sense we'd never have been fooling around, so I guess I did kill her.'

He stood like some ancient penitent in the middle of his accusers, hands by his side palms facing forward. Alysha reached him first the photo frame left behind, she folded him in her arms, just ahead of me and Harry. It probably looked like a footy scrum as we all hugged him.

Alysha spoke quietly, 'I may have come from a different country, but as a dark skinned woman I have lived my life watching white men stare at me since I was a child. Now, with a man like Harry, who had the courage to step out of the crowd and hold my hand, I understand, and I am sure Alice did too.'

Harry had silent tears running down his cheek so did I, I didn't dare look at the rest.

Mum stood up and wrapped her arms around Alysha, looking at Harry and me.

'Now you can understand why it remained a secret for so long. Thank you to Alysha for being the catalyst and letting the demon out. You have arrived with such good credentials. We will all be the happier for having you in our family.'

Alysha smiled as she spoke, 'There is one thing I don't understand. I can figure out which of the men is you,' Alysha said, looking toward Dad, 'I can guess which one was your father, and the Aboriginal staff are pretty self-evident, there are a couple of people almost out of focus plus the horses and dogs, but where is Gran.'

In that split second and with the news Uncle Bart had given me I knew something that we had never done. We had never taken the pictures down and talked about them, what it was all like and who was who.

The small group of black and white images had hung silently on the wall casting long shadows on our lives, as they bleached the timber walls.

'You're very observant,' Mum sighed, looking over at Dad, who was clearly shaken by the question.

'I'm sorry.; Alysha replied, looking to Harry for support.

'What is it Dad?' I spoke into the space created by both my parent's downcast faces.

'Mum I know what it's it all about, we never noticed, but it's plain to see Gran's not there, yet she ought to have been there to farewell her husband and son as they headed into the unknown. Everyone would have been there.'

I both asked and answered the question now hanging in the silent room.

'What are you both so ashamed of, it wasn't you who fell in love with another man, I've read the Coronial enquiry in Uncle Bart's newspapers.'

I heard rather than saw Gran struggle back into the light, suddenly really glad she was still with us, no longer just a feeling of being vaguely happy.

I turned to shuffle across, to be alongside her.

'Can you tell us Gran, or is still painful for you too.' I almost whispered, aware this old secret was going to be hard to bring into the daylight. It had been living in the dark unspoken parts of my family since before Mum and Dad even met. This was really 'The Old Business', the unspoken story behind so much of Dad's behaviour, and I figured, also part of the way Gran was treated.

She smiled, big and lopsided, but in her with-us smile, not a far away one, her gaze and smile focused totally on my face.

'If I don't tell you prob'ly no one ever will. It was my secret you know,' she whispered conspiratorially, looking at me for acknowledgement, seeming unaware of the room full of family who stood or sat breathlessly quiet.

If I tell you you mustn't tell anyone else, someone might get cranky when they hear it all,' she continued in her whisper.

'It will be a secret between us Gran, if you think you are strong enough to tell me the whole story,' knowing I was lying, but determined to get the truth into the light.

'Oohh, I can still do this I think, I don't think I am silly today, but I might need a sweet cuppa tea if you've got one.' She shut her eyes and I thought she'd drifted off again, until she heard the tea tray rattle as Mum put it down on the table alongside her. She did not need to look to know who it was.

'I don't care if you pack me to bed, my Kimberley needs to understand, now this beautiful Alice has come back to be with Harry. She has to know or Alice might tell her but only I really know.'

Mum lifted herself, glanced over Gran's head, first at Dad and then around the room at each of us, aware of everyone. 'It might be a good thing Gran if you feel up to it.'

'Oh I do, no one knows better than me. I do it's been a hard secret to hold all these years, always having to be going to bed early because I was naughty. I don't want to go to bed early anymore, I'm not tired tonight.'

I had no idea what was happening in her mind or where she was going with her memories, but she no longer had that dreamy sound she got when she is off in lala land. The grip she had on my hand was firm, almost too tight, but I let it be.

I wouldn't have done it except my father would never let me have a set of pearls for best dress-up. After I said I would lend him the money dearest Claude said he would get me some. He just needed money to buy more pearl boats. He told me there were lots of pearls in the ocean, but he needed more boats to get them to make enough money for us to get married. Then that horrible storm came.'

She had a long pause and a big sip of her tea, 'Granddad lost his cattle and Claude lost his boats and I got into all the trouble. I hadn't told anyone. If the cyclone hadn't come it would have been alright. No one would have looked for the money because I was the book-keeper. Claude promised he would pay me back.'

Her voice beginning to fade, her cloudy eyes searched my face for understanding her voice almost pleading. 'Claude promised he would marry me and pay it all back. He was going to leave that awful wife, who never came to Broome but always stayed in Paris, in that fancy place she had. Now I'll have to go to bed for being naughty and my dear Bartholemew probably still won't talk to me anymore.'

Her voice began to tail off, thin tears staining her cheeks, I knew she was exhausted, but as she so often had she found a spark. 'I can show you the pearls if you want to see them,' looking at me brightly, searching for my approval.

In turn I searched Mum's face, then Dad's then Harry's, how many more secret were there'

'There aren't any real pearls,' Mum sighed, as if she had heard it all before.

Gran sat forward, to stare hard at her 'You are wrong young miss. You don't know everything. I've hidden them from you all along. In my secret place you could never find them, because I knew you would never let me wear them but Kimberley can see them, because she is never mean to me, and I trust her.' urging me to push her to her room. With Mum shaking her head I went along with her request.

***

Gran's room smelt with the mustiness of a hundred years of darkness of secret times and secrets held tightly. It was redolent with the scent of perfumes long forgotten, the musty smell of old linen stored in cupboards, dancing shoes put away and never used again, through it all was the stale smell of mothballs gone to dust. Like an invisible powder the odour hung thickly, mixed with the dust of endless brush strokes as Gran searched each night for her once good looks.

I had gone there as a child, but not for years, it had forever been Mum's or sis's job to put Gran to bed.

For me it was a forgotten room.

The same heavy brocaded curtains I remembered, hung still half closed, the same quilted cotton bedspread looking its age, and the amoire or European clothes cupboard that some ancestor had carted half way around the world was still standing against the far wall, still looking elegant, if chipped.

Gran took control of her wheelchair and with a sudden strength pushed herself to the cedar chest, next to the amoire, opening one of its three lids with her good arm as she did.

I stood back not sure I wanted the answer.

I could hear her rummaging around in the piles of fabrics jumbled on the floor of the beautiful old cedar clothes chest then I heard a muffled but distinct 'click'.

In seconds she held it out triumphantly.

A beautiful slim dark wooden jewelry box.

With a conspiratorial crook of her index finger she beckoned me over.

'Look at them', breathing heavily, 'one set is not just paste real, these ones are worth half a million pounds in Europe, each one picked out of pearl shells from the clean ocean sands in Broome by Claude's divers. Each one opened on the rolling deck of his lead boat. He had several boats you know, but he needed more to find more pearls to earn enough for us to be married.'

She looked up at me with pride.

'Claude chose every single one and paid for the paste set to be made. He had the pearls strung just for me, aren't they magnificent, they'll be yours when I die.

I bent to kiss her powdered, aged forehead, aware as I did it might be my last kiss.

'They are wonderful Gran just magnificent. He must have loved you a lot.'

'Oh yes he did my dear, Claude was smitten with me,if it had not been for that wife of his in Paris and of course your Granddad we would have made it public.

But we never did.'

She stared up at me with hope in her eyes, As I looked back I realised how cloudy age had made them.

'I just knew you would understand. No one else does.'

I backed out of the room, leaving her dozing in her ocean of memories. A little unsteadily I made my way back to the lounge where everyone waited, cups of tea all gone cold.

'You were right Mum they are stage pearls. The paste is all cracked and shows the plastic. But I couldn't tell her, she cradled them like she was holding the crown jewels. She has dozed off in her chair. I put the brakes on. She won't get hurt.'

As one we left the lounge. Left Gran sleeping and walked outside, to just breathe the cooler air the lounge was stifling and we all needed to stretch.

Harry spoke first. 'Alysha and I have to go back North, we promised, but we'll come back here as soon as we can. I think given time we both reckon we can make a go of it here, especially with Bert's money, eh Alysha,' who smiled coyly and held his hand, muttering something sweet as they hugged, before turning to look at me.

'I just have to cut a couple of hard years out, win the School Prefect Award, the Cross Country cup and make friends with a great bunch of kids and I'll be back. So then it will just be up to Sis to decide where she wants to camp.'

As I looked around I realised she was still in bed.

'That's if she learns to get up early enough. What I need to do right now is to go over to Jamieson's to say hello to Bop. If she smells I've been here and haven't been to see her she'll divorce me or whatever dogs do to owners, Harry you and Aly should come over too. Harry you need to meet Paulz, she's probably home and Aly you'll love the homestead. Anyway I'm taking Bert's old Landrover so there's plenty of room, if you don't mind the drafts.

Harry turned to look at the homestead, then took a long look at the love of his life. 'What do you reckon Aly, like to come and see a bit more of the place. We've done the homestead and you've heard the worst of our secrets, this might be where we live.'

Her wide smile said Harry could have suggested a trip to Hades and she would have followed him, dog paddling down the Styx.

I answered for her. 'Ok let's go, Gran will wake up some time, then it will get a bit more complicated to get away and drive over.'

The drive over was fun, squeezed into the front bench seat we swapped yarns and joked as we bumped around in the rattly Landrover, memories of Bert all through it.

Alysha must have begun to realize how close Harry and I were as we teased each other relentlessly. I hadn't rung ahead so wasn't sure Paulz would be there, but I wanted a look around now the place was bare of all that had been sold at Auction, and I knew Paulz was camping in the old overseer's house not the homestead. I'd taken off as soon as the auction was over to give my new possession a run and had only been over with Dad since to look around the paddocks.

While I ran toward the kennels where Bop was chained, Harry and Aly headed towards the Jamieson's homestead. It took me a minute to free Bop from the chain which had become tangled as she leapt about in her excitement. Her ruckus had started as soon as she smelt me and only got louder as I briefly talked to Harry. Her barking and yelping left me in no doubt that she remembered me and was pretty keen to catch up on what all my new smells meant. I wasn't sure who was most excited Bop or me. I got teary as she jumped all over me, which had been a no-no when she was a pup. Going back to Mt Macedon was quickly not looking like such a fun thing without Bop. I was sitting on some grass and rubbing her tummy, scratching her ears and asking her what she had been doing while I was away, when a forgotten voice over my shoulder made look back.

Turning I found Paulz almost on top of us, she'd walked up unheard due to the noise Bop and I were making. 'Obviously pretty glad to see you, hasn't forgotten you has she.'

Paulz grin said he was glad Bop hadn't immediately run to him but stayed playing with me. 'Harry was right, she still remembers you, she works each day with me and has not developed a single bad habit while you've been away. All she wants to do each morning is get into the paddocks, work the mobs and spend time in the yards. You can go back to school confident she'll be waiting for you when you come home each term break.'

On his invite to have a cuppa we walked together back to Paulz house, with Bop doing circles around us continuing her excited din. Before we got there Harry and Alysha emerged from the homestead.

I introduced them, 'Paulz this is my big brother Harry and his fiancé Alysha'.

'Would you like to join us in a cuppa, my house is tidy and I have some Anzac biscuits hot out of the oven that you're welcome to share.'

As I'd suspected Harry and Paulz got on instantly, discussing machinery, cars and bikes. Asking Paulz if it was ok Alysha and I went for a tour of the Jamieson's old overseer's house.

It was clean, reasonably large, had four bedrooms, two bathrooms and a billiard room. The kitchen was a bit old fashioned but had a decent AGA, an electric range and heaps of bench space. There were two large bay windows that between them overlooked the veggie garden and the drive. I could see myself living there later in life, Alysha sharing my view. When we walked back into the lounge the boys were winding down, so it was easy to suggest we headed back to Walkaway and dinner.

***

Sitting around the dining table with a feast Mum had just knocked up I looked towards Gran's room where I presumed she was still fast asleep and remembered something she used to say. 'Life is truly like one long sentence. Words and more words, mainly separated by commas, with some exclamation marks, if you're lucky a semi colon or three, always lots of question marks, but only one real full stop.'

www.ingramcontent.com/pod-product-compliance
Lightning Source LLC
LaVergne TN
LVHW051003080826
845145LV00009B/2438

* 9 7 8 0 6 4 5 7 9 5 8 9 9 *